THE GENIAL IDIOT

HIS VIEWS AND REVIEWS

THE GENIAL IDIOT

HIS VIEWS AND REVIEWS

JOHN KENDRICK BANGS

WILDSIDE PRESS

THE GENIAL IDIOT

Published by Wildside Press LLC.
www.wildsidebooks.com

CONTENTS

CHAPTER I

HE DISCUSSES MAXIMS AND PROVERBS

"GOOD!" cried the Idiot, from behind the voluminous folds of the magazine section of his Sunday newspaper. "Here's a man after my own heart. Professor Duff, of Glasgow University, has come out with a public statement that the maxims and proverbs of our forefathers are largely hocus-pocus and buncombe. I've always maintained that myself from the moment I had my first copy-book lesson in which I had to scrawl the line, 'It's a long lane that has no turning,' twenty-four times. And then that other absurd statement, 'A stitch in the side is worth two in the hand'—or something like it—I forget just how it goes—what Tommy-rot that is."

"Well, I don't know about that, Mr. Idiot," said Mr. Whitechoker, tapping his fingers together reflectively. "Certain great moral principles are instilled into the minds of the young by the old proverbs and maxims that remain with them forever, and become a potent influence in the formation of character."

"I should like to agree with you, but I can't," said the Idiot. "I don't believe anything that is noble in the way of character was ever fostered by such a statement as that it's a long lane that has no turning. In the first place, it isn't necessarily true. I know a lane on my grandfather's farm that led from the hen-coop to the barn. There wasn't a turn nor a twist in it, and I know by actual measurement that it wasn't sixty feet long. You've got just as much right to say to a boy that it's a long nose that has no twisting, or a long leg that has no pulling, or a long courtship that has no kissing. There's infinitely more truth in those last two than in the original model. The leg that's never pulled doesn't go short in a stringent financial market, and a courtship without a kiss, even if it lasted only five minutes, would be too long for any self-respecting lover."

"I never thought of it in that way," said Mr. Whitechoker. "Perhaps, after all, the idea is ill-expressed in the original."

"Perfectly correct," said the Idiot. "But even then, what? Suppose they had put the thing right in the beginning and said 'it's a long lane that has no ending.' What's the use of putting a thing like that in a copy-book? A boy who didn't know that without being told ought to be spanked and put to bed. Why not tell him it's a long well that has no bottom, or a long dog that has no wagging, or a long railroad that has no terminal facilities?"

"Oh, well," interposed the Bibliomaniac, "what's the use of being captious? Out of a billion and a half wise saws you pick out one to jump on. Because one is weak, all the rest must come down with a crash."

"There are plenty of others, and the way they refute one another is to me a constant source of delight," said the Idiot. "There's 'Procrastination is the thief of time,' for instance. That's a clear injunction to youth to get up and hustle, and he starts in with all the impulsiveness of youth, and the first thing he knows—bang! he runs slap into 'Look before you leap,' or 'Second thoughts are best.' That last is what Samuel Johnson would have called a beaut. What superior claims the second thought has over the first or the seventy-seventh thought, that it should become axiomatic, I vow I can't see. If it's morality you're after I am dead against the teachings of that proverb. The second thought is the open door to duplicity when it comes to a question of morals. You ask a small boy, who has been in swimming when he ought to have been at Sunday-school, why his shirt is wet. His first thought is naturally to reply along the line of fact and say, 'Why, because it fell into the pond.' But second thought comes along with visions of hard spanking and a supperless bed in store for him, and suggests the idea that 'There was a leak in the Sunday-school roof right over the place where I was sitting,' or, 'I sat down on the teacher's glass of water.' That's the sort of thing second thought does in the matter of morals.

"I admit, of course, that there are times when second thoughts are better than first ones—for instance, if your first thought is to name the baby Jimmie and Jimmie turns out to be a girl, it is better to obey your second thought and call her Gladys or Samantha—but it is not always so, and I object to the nerve of the broad, general statement that it *is* so. Sometimes fifth thoughts are best. In science I guess you'll find that the man who thinks the seven hundred and ninety-seventh thought along certain lines has got the last and best end of it. And so it goes—out of the infinitesimal number of numbers, every mother's son of 'em may at the psychological moment have a claim to the supremacy, but your self-sufficient old proverb-maker falls back behind the impenetrable wall of his own conceit, and announces that because he has nothing but second-hand thoughts, therefore the second thought is best, and we, like a flock of sheep, follow this leader, and go blatting that sentiment down through the ages as if it were proved beyond peradventure by the sum total of human experience."

"Well, you needn't get mad about it," said the Lawyer. "I never said it—so you can't blame me."

"Still, there are some proverbs," said Mr. Whitechoker, blandly, "that we may not so summarily dismiss. Take, for instance, 'You never miss the water till the well runs dry.'"

"One of the worst of the lot, Mr. Whitechoker," said the Idiot. "I've missed the water lots of times when the well was full as ever. You miss the water when the pipes freeze up, don't you? You—or rather I—I sometimes miss the water like time at five o'clock in the morning after a pleasant evening with some jovial friends, when there's no end of it in the well, but not a drop within reach of my fevered hand, and I haven't the energy to grope my way down-stairs to the ice-pitcher. There's more water in that proverb than tangible assets. From the standpoint of veracity that's one of the most immoral proverbs of the lot—and if you came to apply it to the business world—oh, Lud! As a rule, these days, you never *find* the water till the well has been pumped dry and put in the hands of a receiver for the benefit of the bond-holders. Fact is, all these water proverbs are to be regarded with suspicion."

"I don't recall any other," said Mr. Whitechoker.

"Well," said the Idiot, "there's one, and it's the nerviest of 'em all—'Water never runs up hill.' Ask any man in Wall Street how high the water has run up in the last five years and see what he tells you. And then, 'You may drive a horse to water, but you cannot make him drink,' is another choice specimen of the Waterbury School of Philosophy. I know a lot of human horses who have been driven to water lately, and such drinkers as they have become! It's really awful. If I knew the name of that particular Maximilian who invented those water proverbs I'd do my best to have him indicted for doing business without a license."

"It's very unfortunate," said Mr. Whitechoker, "that modern conditions should so have upset the wisdom of the ancients."

"It is too bad," said the Idiot. "And I am just as sorry about it as you are; but, after all, the wisdom of the ancients, wise and wisdomatic as it was, should not be permitted to put at nought all modern thought. Why not adapt the wisdom of the ancients to modern conditions? You can't begin too soon, for new generations are constantly springing up, and I know of no better outlet for reform than in these self-same Spencerian proverbs which the poor kids have to copy, copy, copy, until they are sick and tired of them. Now, in the writing-lessons, why not adapt your means to your ends? Why make a beginner in penmanship write over and over again, 'A bird in the hand is worth two in the bush?'—which it isn't, by-the-way, to a man who is a good shot—when you can bear in on his mind that 'A dot on the I is worth two on the T'; or, for the instruction of your school-teachers, why don't you get up a proverb like 'It's a long lesson that has no learning'? Or if you are interested in having your boy brought up to the strenuous life, why don't you have him make sixty copies of the aphorism, 'A punch in the solar is worth six on the nose?' You tell your children never to whistle until they are out of the woods. Now, where in the name of all that's lovely should a boy whistle if not in the woods? That's where birds whistle. That's where the wind whistles. If nature whistles anywhere, it is in the woods. Woods were made for whistling, and any man who ever sat over a big log-fire in camp or in library who has not noticed that the logs themselves whistle constantly—well, he is a pachyderm."

"Well, as far as I can reach a conclusion from all that you have said," put in Mr. Whitechoker, "the point seems to be that the proverbs of the ancients are not suited to modern conditions, and that you think they should be revised."

"Exactly," said the Idiot.

"It's a splendid idea," said Mr. Brief. "But, after all, you've got to have something to begin on. Possibly," he added, with a wink at the Bibliomaniac, "you have a few concrete examples to show us what can be done."

"Certainly," said the Idiot. "Here is a list of them."

And as he rose up to depart he handed Mr. Brief a paper on which he had written as follows:

"You never find the water till the stock falls off twenty points."
"A stitch in time saves nothing at all at present tailors' rates."
"You look after the pennies. Somebody else will deposit the
    pounds."
"It's a long heiress that knows no yearning."
"Second thoughts are always second."
"Procrastination is the theme of gossips."
"Never put off to-day what you can put on day after to-morrow."
"Sufficient unto the day are the obligations of last month."
"One good swat deserves another."

"By Jove!" said Mr. Brief, as he read them off, "you can't go back on any of 'em, can you?"

"No," said the Bibliomaniac; "that's the great trouble with the Idiot. Even with all his idiocy he is not always a perfect idiot."

CHAPTER II

HE DISCUSSES THE IDEAL HUSBAND

"WELL, I see the Ideal Husband has broken out again," said the Idiot, after reading a short essay on that interesting but rare individual by Gladys Waterbury Shrivelton of the Woman's Page of the Squehawkett *Gazoo*. "I'd hoped they had him locked up for good, he's been so little in evidence of late years."

"Why should you wish so estimable an individual to be locked up?" demanded Mr. Pedagog, who, somehow or other, seemed to take the Idiot's suggestion as personal.

"To keep his idealness from being shattered," said the Idiot. "Nothing against the gentleman himself, I can assure you. It would be a pity, I think, once you have really found an Ideal Husband, to subject him to the coarse influences of the world; to let him go forth into the madding crowd and have the sweet idyllic bloom rubbed off by the attritions of the vulgar. I feel about the Ideal Husband just as I do about a beautiful peachblow vase which is too fragile, too delicate to be brought into contact with the ordinary earthen-ware of society. The earthen-ware isn't harmed by bumping into the peachblow, but the peachblow will inevitably turn up with a crack here and a nick there and a hole somewhere else after such an encounter. If I were a woman and suddenly discovered that I had an Ideal Husband, I think at my personal sacrifice I'd present him to the Metropolitan Museum of Art or immure him in some other retreat where his perfection would remain forever secure—say, up among the Egyptian mummies of the British Museum. We cannot be too careful, Mr. Pedagog, of these rarely beautiful things that are now and again vouchsafed to us."

"What is an Ideal Husband, anyhow?" asked Mr. Brief. "Has the recipe for such an individual at last been discovered?"

"Yes," put in Mrs. Pedagog, before the Idiot had a chance to reply, and here the dear old landlady fixed her eyes firmly and affectionately upon her spouse, the school-master. "I can tell you the recipe for the Ideal Husband. Years, sixty-three—"

"Sixty-two, my dear," smiled Mr. Pedagog, "and—er—a fraction—verging on sixty-three."

"Years, verging on sixty-three," said Mrs. Pedagog, accepting the correction. "Character developed by time and made secure. Eyes, blue; disposition when vexed, vexatious; disposition when pleased, happy; irritable from just cause; considerate always; calm exterior, heart of gold;

prompt in anger and quick in forgiveness; and only one old woman in the world for him."

"A trifle bald-headed, but a true friend when needed, eh?" said the Idiot.

"I try to be," said Mr. Pedagog, pleasantly complacent.

"Well, you succeed in both," said the Idiot.

"For your trifling baldness is evident when you remove your hat, which, like a true gentleman, you never fail to do at the breakfast-table, and, after a fifteen years' experience with you, I for one can say that I have found you always the true friend when I needed you—I never told how, without my solicitation and entirely upon your own initiative, you once loaned me the money to pay Mrs. Pedagog's bill over which she was becoming anxious."

"John," cried Mrs. Pedagog, severely, "did you ever do that?"

"Well, my dear—er—only once, you know, and you were so re-lieved—" began Mr. Pedagog.

"You should have lent the money to me, John," said Mrs. Pedagog, "and then I should not have been compelled to dun the Idiot."

"I know, my dear, but you see I knew the Idiot would pay me back, and perhaps—well, only perhaps, my love—you might not have thought of it," explained the school-master, with a slight show of embarrassment.

"The Ideal Husband is ever truthful, too," said the landlady, with a smile as broad as any.

"Well, it's too bad, I think," said the Lawyer, "that a man has to be verging on sixty-three to be an Ideal Husband. I'm only forty-four, and I should hate to think that if I should happen to get married within the next two or three years my wife would have to wait at least fifteen years before she could find me all that I ought to be. Moreover, I have been told that I have black eyes."

"With the unerring precision of a trained legal mind," said the Idiot, "you have unwittingly put your finger on the crux of the whole matter, Mr. Brief. Mrs. Pedagog has been describing *her* Ideal Husband, and I am delighted to know that what I have always suspected to be the case is in fact the truth: that *her* husband in her eyes is an ideal one. That's the way it ought to be, and that is why we have always found her the sweet-est of landladies, but because Mrs. Pedagog prefers Mr. Pedagog in this race for supremacy in the domain of a woman's heart is no reason why you who are only bald-headed in your temper, like most of us, should not prove to be equally the ideal of some other woman—in fact, of several others. Women are not all alike. As a matter of fact, a gentleman named Balzac, who was the Marie Corelli of his age in France, once committed himself to the inference that no two women ever were alike, so that, if you grant the truth of old Balzac's inference, the Ideal Husband will probably vary to the extent of the latest count of the number of women in the world. So why give up hope because you are only forty-nine?"

"Forty-four," corrected the Lawyer.

"Pardon me—forty-four," said the Idiot. "When you are in the roaring forties, five or six years more or less do not really count. Lots of men who are really only forty-two behave like sixty, and I know one old duffer of forty-nine who has the manners of eighteen. The age question does not really count."

"No—you are proof of that," said the Bibliomaniac. "You have been twenty-four years old for the last fifteen years."

"Thank you, Mr. Bib," said the Idiot. "You are one of the few people in the world who really understand me. I have tried to be twenty-four for the past fifteen years, and if I have succeeded, so much the better for me. It's a beautiful age. You feel that you know so much when you're twenty-four. If it should turn out to be the answer to 'How old is Ann?' the lady should be congratulated. But, as a matter of fact, you can be an Ideal Husband at any old age."

"Humph! At seven, for instance?" drawled Mr. Brief.

"Seven is not any old age," retorted the Idiot. "It is a very certain old youth. Nor does it depend upon the color of the eyes, so long as they are neither green nor red. Nobody could ever make an Ideal Husband out of a green-eyed man, or a chap given to the red eye, either—"

"It all depends upon the kind of a man you are, eh?" said the Bibliomaniac.

"Not a bit of it," said the Idiot. "It depends on the kind of wife you've got, and that's why I say that the Ideal Husband varies to the extent of the latest count of the women in the world. Take the case of Mr. Pedagog here. Mrs. Pedagog accuses him of being an Ideal Husband, and he, without any attempt at evasion, acknowledges the corn, like the honorable gentleman he is. But can you imagine Mr. Pedagog being an Ideal Husband to some lady in the Four Hundred, with a taste for grand opera that strikes only on the box; with a love for Paris gowns that are worth a fortune; with the midnight supper and cotillion after habit firmly intrenched in her character; with an ambition to shine all summer at Newport, all autumn at Lenox, all winter at New York, with a dash to England and France in the merry, merry springtime? Do you suppose our friend John Pedagog here would be in it with Tommie Goldilocks Van Varick as the Ideal Husband of such a woman? Not on your life. Well, then, take Tommie Goldilocks Van Varick, who'd be the Ideal Spouse of this brilliant social light Mrs. Van Varick. How would he suit Mrs. Pedagog, rising at eleven-thirty every day and yelling like mad for the little blue bottle which clears the head from the left-over cobwebs of yesterday; eating his egg and drinking his coffee with a furrow in his brow almost as deep as the pallor of his cheek, and now and then making a most awful grimace because the interior of his mouth feels like a bargain day at the fur-counter of a department store; spending his afternoon sitting in the window of the Hunky Dory Club ogling the passers-by and making bets on such important questions as whether more hansoms pass up the Avenue than down, or whether the proportion of red-haired girls to white horses is as great between three and four P.M. as between five and six—"

"I don't see how a woman could stand a man like that," said Mrs. Pedagog. "Indeed, I don't see where his ideal qualities come in, anyhow, Mr. Idiot. I think you are wrong in putting him among the Ideal Husbands even for Mrs. Van Varick."

"No, I am not wrong, for he is indeed the very essence of her ideal because he doesn't make her stand him," said the Idiot. "He never bothers Mrs. Van Varick at all. On the first of every month he sends her a check for a good round sum with which she can pay her bills. He presents her with a town house and a country house, and a Limousine car, and all the furs she can possibly want; provides her with an opera-box, and never fails, when he himself goes to the opera, to call upon her and pay his respects like a gentleman. If she sustains heavy losses at bridge, he makes them good, and when she gives a dinner to her set, or to some distinguished social lion from other zoos, Van Varick is always on hand to do the honors of his house, and what is supposed to be his table. He and Mrs. Van Varick are on the most excellent terms; in fact, he treats her with more respect than he does any other woman he knows, never even suggesting the idea of a flirtation with her. In other words, he does not interfere with her in any way, which is the only kind of man in the world she could be happy with."

"It's perfectly awful!" cried Mrs. Pedagog. "If they never see each other, what on earth did they ever get married for?"

"Protection," said the Idiot. "And it is perfectly splendid in its results. Mrs. Van Varick, being married to so considerate an absentee, is able to go about very much as she pleases backed with the influence and affluence of the Van Varick name. This as plain little Miss Floyd Poselthwaite she was unable to do. She has now an assured position, and is protected against the chance of marrying a man who, unlike Van Varick, would growl at her expenditures, object to her friends, and insist upon coming home to dinner every night, and occasionally turn up at breakfast."

"Sweet life," said the Bibliomaniac. "And what does the Willieboy husband get out of it?"

"Pride, protection, and freedom," said the Idiot. "He's as proud as Punch when he sees Mrs. Van V. swelling about town with her name kept as standing matter in every society column in the country. His freedom he enjoys, just as she enjoys hers. If he doesn't turn up for six weeks she never asks any questions, and so Van Varick can live on easy terms with the truth. If he sits up all night over a game of cards, there's nobody to chide him for doing so, and—"

"But where does his protection come in? That's what I can't see," said the Bibliomaniac.

"It's as plain as a pike-staff," said the Idiot. "With Mrs. Van Varick on the *tapis*, Tommie is safe from designing ladies who might marry him for his money."

"Well, he's a mighty poor ideal!" cried Mr. Pedagog.

"He certainly would not do for Mrs. Pedagog," said the Idiot. "But you would yourself be no better for Mrs. Van Varick. The red Indian makes an Ideal Husband for the squaw, but he'd never suit a daughter of the British nobility any more than the Duke of Lacklands would make a good husband for dusky little Minnehaha. So I say what's the use of discussing the matter any further with the purpose of arbitrarily settling on what it is that constitutes an Ideal Husband? We may all hope to be considered such if we only find the girl that likes our particular kind."

"Then," said Mr. Brief, with a smile, "your advice to me is not to despair, eh?"

"That's it," said the Idiot. "I wouldn't give up, if I were you. There's no telling when some one will come along to whom you appear to be the perfect creature."

"Good!" cried Mr. Brief. "You are mighty kind. I don't suppose you can give me a hint as to how soon I may expect to meet the lady?"

"Well—no, I can't," said the Idiot. "I don't believe even Edison could tell you about when to look for arrivals from Mars."

CHAPTER III

THE IDIOT'S VALENTINE

"WELL, old man," said the Poet, as the Idiot entered the breakfast-room on the morning of Valentine's day, "how did old St. Valentine treat you? Any results worth speaking of?"

"Oh, the usual lay-out," returned the Idiot, languidly. "Nine hundred and forty-two passionate declarations of undying affection from unknown lady friends in all parts of the civilized world; one thousand three hundred and twenty-four highly colored but somewhat insulting intimations that I had better go 'way back and sit down from hitherto unsuspected gentlemen friends scattered from Maine to California; one small can of salt marked 'St. Valentine to the Idiot,' with sundry allusions to the proper medical treatment of the latter's freshness, and a small box containing a rubber bottle-stopper labelled 'Cork up and bust.' I can't complain."

"Well, you did come in for your share of it, didn't you?" said Mr. Brief.

"Yes," said the Idiot, "I think I got all that was coming to me, and I wouldn't have minded it if I hadn't had to pay three dollars over-due postage on 'em. I don't bother much if some anonymous chap off in the wilds of Kalikajoo takes the trouble to send me a funny picture of a monkey grinding a hand-organ with 'the loving regards of your brother,' or if somebody else who is afraid of becoming too fond of me sends me a horse-chestnut with a line to the effect that here is one I haven't printed, I don't feel like getting mad; but when I have to pay the postage on the plaguey things it strikes me it is rubbing it in a little too hard, and if I could find two or three of the senders I'd spend an hour or two of my time banging their heads together."

"I got off pretty well," said the Bibliomaniac. "I only got one valentine, and though it cast some doubt upon the quality of my love for books, I found it quite amusing. I'll read it to you."

Here the Bibliomaniac took a small paper from his pocket and read the following lines:

"THE HUNGRY BIBLIOMANIAC

"If only you would cut your books
As often as your butter,
When people ask you what's inside

You wouldn't sit and sputter.
The reading that hath made you full,
The reading that doth chain you,
Is not from books, or woman's looks,
But fresh from off the menu."

"What do you think of that?" asked the Bibliomaniac, with a chuckle, as he folded up his valentine and stowed it away in his pocket once more.

"I think I can spot the sender," said the Idiot, fixing his eyes sternly upon the Poet. "It takes genius to get up a rhyme like 'men' and 'chain you,' and I know of only one man at this board or at any other who is equal to the task."

"If you mean me," retorted the Poet, flushing, "you are mightily mistaken. I wouldn't waste a rhyme like that on a personal valentine when I could tack it on to the end of a sonnet and go out and sell it for two-fifty."

"Then you didn't do it, eh?" demanded the Idiot.

"No. Did you?" asked the Poet, with his eyes twinkling.

"Sir," said the Idiot, "if I had done it, would I have had the unblushing effrontery to say, as I just now did say, that its author was a genius?"

"Well, we're square, anyhow," said the Poet. "You cast me under suspicion, to begin with, and it was only fair that I should whack back. I got a valentine myself, and I suspect it was from the same hand. It runs like this:

"TO THE MINOR POET

"You do not pluck the fairy flowers
That bloom on high Parnassus,
Nor do you gather thistles like
Some of those mystic asses
Who browse about old Helicon
In hope to fill their tummies;
Yours rather are those dandy-lines—
Gilt-topped chrysanthemummies—
Quite pleasant stuff
That ends in fluff—
Yet when they are beholden
Make all the world look golden."

"Well," ejaculated the Idiot, "I don't see what there is in that to make you angry. Seems to me there's some very nice compliments in that. For instance, your stuff when 'tis

'beholden
Makes all the world look golden,'

according to your anonymous correspondent. If he'd been vicious he might have said something like this:

'—withal so supercilious
They make the whole earth bilious.'"

The Poet grinned. "I'm not complaining about it. It's a mighty nice little verse, I think, and my only regret is that I do not know who the chap was who sent it. I'd like to thank him. I had an idea you might help me," he said, with a searching glance.

"I will," said the Idiot. "If the man who sent you that ever reveals his identity to me I will tell him you fell all over yourself with joy on receiving his tribute of admiration. How did you come out, Doctor?"

"Oh, he remembered me, all right," said the Doctor. "Quite in the same vein, too, only he's not so complimentary. He calls me 'The Humane Surgeon,' and runs into rhyme after this fashion:

"O, Doctor Blank's a surgeon bold,
A surgeon most humane, sir;
And what he does is e'er devoid
Of ordinary pain, sir.

"If he were called to amputate
A leg hurt by a bullet,
He wouldn't take a knife and cut—
But with his bill he'd pull it."

"He must have had some experience with you, Doctor," said the Idiot. "In fact, he knows you so well that I am inclined to think that the writer of that valentine lives in this house, and it is just possible that the culprit is seated at this table at this moment."

"I think it very likely," said the Doctor, dryly. "He's a fresh young man, five feet ten inches in height—"

"Pooh—pooh!" said the Idiot. "That's the worst description of Mr. Brief I ever heard. Mr. Brief, in the first place, is not a young man, and he isn't fresh—"

"I didn't mean Mr. Brief," said the Doctor, significantly.

"Then you ought to be ashamed of yourself to intimate that Mr. Whitechoker, a clergyman, would stoop to the writing of such a rhyme as that," cried the Idiot. "People nowadays seem to me to be utterly lacking in that respect for the cloth to which it is entitled. Mr. Brief, if you really wrote that thing you owe it to Mr. Whitechoker to own up and thus relieve him of the suspicion the Doctor has so unblushingly cast upon him."

"I can prove an alibi," said the Lawyer. "I could no more turn a rhyme than I could play 'Parsifal' on a piano with one finger, and I wouldn't if I could. I judge, from what I know of the market value of poems these days, that that valentine of the Doctor's is worth about two dollars. It would take me a century to write it, and inasmuch as my time is worth at least five dollars a year it stands to reason that I would not put in five hundred dollars' worth of effort on a two-dollar job. So that lets me out. By-the-way, I got one of these trifles myself. Want to hear it?"

"I am just crazy to hear it," said the Idiot. "If any man has reduced you to poetry, Mr. Brief, he's a great man. With all your many virtues, you seem to me to fit into a poetical theme about as snugly as an automobile with full power on in a china-shop. By all means let us have it."

"This modern St. Valentine of ours has reduced the profession to verse with a nicety that elicits my most profound admiration," said Mr. Brief. "Just listen to this:

"The Lawyer is no wooer, yet
To sue us is his whim.
The Lawyer is no tailor, but
We get our suits from him.
The longest things in all the world—
They are the Lawyer's briefs,
And all the joys he gets in life
Are other people's griefs.
Yet spite of all the Lawyer's faults
He's one point rather nice:
He'll not remain lest you retain
And never gives advice."

"The author of these valentines," said the Doctor, "is to be spotted, the way I diagnose the case, by his desire that professional people should be constantly giving away their services. He objects to the Doctor's bill and he slaps sarcastically at the Lawyer because he doesn't *give* advice. That's why I suspect the Idiot. He's a professional Idiot, and yet he gives his idiocy away."

"When did I ever give myself away?" demanded the Idiot. "You are talking wildly, Doctor. The idea of your trying to drag me into this thing is preposterous. Suppose you show down your valentine and see if it is in my handwriting."

"Mine is typewritten," said the Doctor.

"So is mine," said the Bibliomaniac.

"Mine, too," said the Poet.

"Same here," said Mr. Brief.

"Well, then," said the Idiot, "I'm willing to write a page in my own hand without any attempt to disguise it, and let any handwriting expert decide as to whether there is the slightest resemblance between my chirography and these typewritten sheets you hold in your hand."

"That's fair enough," said Mr. Whitechoker.

"Besides," persisted the Idiot, "I've received one of the things myself, and it'll make your hair curl, if you've got any. Typewritten like the rest of 'em. Shall I read it?"

By common consent the Idiot read the following:

> *"Idiot, zany, brain of hare,*
> *Dolt and noodle past compare,*
> *Buncombe, bosh, and verbal slosh,*
> *Mind of nothing, full of josh,*
> *Madman, donkey, dizzard-pate,*
> *U. S. Zero Syndicate,*
> *Dull, depressing, lack of wit,*
> *Incarnation of the nit.*
> *Minus, numskull, drivelling baby,*
> *Greenhorn, dunce, and dotard Gaby;*
> *All the queer and loony chorus*
> *Found in old Roget's Thesaurus,*
> *Flat and crazy through and through,*
> *That, O Idiot—that is you.*
> *Let me tell you, sir, in fine,*
> *I won't be your Valentine.*

"What do you think of that?" asked the Idiot, when he had finished. "Wouldn't that jar you?"

"I think it's perfectly horrid," said Mrs. Pedagog. "Mary, pass the pancakes to the Idiot. Mr. Idiot, let me hand you a full cup of coffee. John, hand the Idiot the syrup. Why, how a thing like that should be allowed to go through the mails passes me!"

And the others all agreed that the landlady's indignation was justified, because they were fond of the Idiot in spite of his faults. They would not see him abused, at any rate.

* * * *

"Say, old man," said the Poet, later, "I really thought you sent those other valentines until you read yours."

"I thought you would," said the Idiot. "That's the reason why I worked up that awful one on myself. That relieves me of all suspicion."

CHAPTER IV

HE DISCUSSES FINANCE

A MESSENGER had just brought a "collect" telegram for the Doctor, and that gentleman, after going through all his pockets, and finding nothing but a bunch of keys and a prescription-pad, made the natural inquiry:

"Anybody got a quarter?"

"I have," said the Idiot. "One of the rare mintage of 1903, circulated for a short time only and warranted good as new."

"I didn't know the 1903 quarter was rare," said the Bibliomaniac, who prided himself on being a numismatist of rare ability. "Who told you the 1903 quarter was rare?"

"My old friend, Experience," said the Idiot.

"What's rare about it?" demanded the Bibliomaniac.

"Why—it's what they call ready money, spot cash, the real thing with the water squeezed out, selling at par on sight," explained the Idiot. "Millions of people never saw one, and under modern conditions it is very difficult to amass them in any considerable quantity. What is worse, even if you happen to get one of them it is next to impossible to hang on to it without unusual effort. If you have a 1903 quarter in your pocket, somehow or other the idea that it is in your possession seems to communicate itself to others, and every effort is made to lure it away from you on some pretext or other."

"Excuse me for interrupting this lecture of yours, Mr. Idiot," said the Doctor, amiably, "but would you mind lending me that quarter to pay this messenger? I've left my change in my other clothes."

"What did I tell you?" cried the Idiot, triumphantly. "The words are no sooner out of my mouth than they are verified. Hardly a minute elapses from the time Doctor Capsule learns that I have that quarter before he puts in an application for it."

"Well, I renew the application in spite of its rarity," laughed the Doctor. "It's even rarer with me than it is with you. Shell out—there's a good chap."

"I will if you'll put up a dollar for security," said the Idiot, extracting the coin from his pocket, "and give me a demand note at thirty days for the quarter."

"I haven't got a dollar," said the Doctor.

"Well, what other collateral have you to offer?" asked the Idiot. "I won't take buckwheat-cakes, or muffins, or your share of the sausages, mind you. They come under the head of wild-cat securities—here to-day and gone to-morrow."

"My, but you're a Shylock!" ejaculated Mr. Brief.

"Not a bit of it," retorted the Idiot. "If I were Shylock I'd be willing to take a steak for security, but there's none of the pound of flesh business about me. I simply proceed cautiously, like any modern financial institution that intends to stay in the ring more than two weeks. I'm not one of your fortnightly trust companies with an oak table, an unpaid bill for office rent, and a patent reversible disappearing president for its assets. I do business on the national-bank principle: millions for the rich, but not one cent for the man that needs the money."

"I tell you what I'll do," said the Doctor. "If you'll lend me that quarter, I won't charge you a cent for my professional services next time you need them."

"That's a large offer, but I'm afraid of it," replied the Idiot. "It partakes of the nature of a speculation. It's dealing in futures, which is not a safe thing for a financial institution to do, I don't care how solid it is. You don't catch the Chemistry National Bank lending money to anybody on mere prospects, and, what is more, in my case, I'd have to get sick to win out. No, Doctor, that proposition does not appeal to me."

"Looks hopeless, doesn't it," said the Doctor. "Mary, tell the boy to wait while I run up-stairs—"

"I wouldn't do that," said the Idiot, interrupting. "The matter can be arranged in another way. I honestly don't like to lend money, believing with Polonius that it's a bad thing to do. As the Governor of North Carolina said to the Governor of South Carolina, who owed him a hundred dollars, 'It's a long time between payments on account,' and that sort of thing breaks up families, not to mention friendships. But I will match you for it."

"How can I match when I haven't anything to match with?" said the Doctor, growing a trifle irritable.

"You can match your credit against my quarter," said the Idiot. "We can make it a mental match—a sort of Christian Science gamble. What am I thinking of, heads or tails?"

"Heads," said the Doctor.

"By Jove, that's hard luck!" ejaculated the Idiot. "You lose. I was thinking of tails."

"Oh, thunder!" cried the Doctor, impatiently.

"Try it again, double or quits. What am I thinking of?" said the Idiot.

"Heads," repeated the Doctor.

"Somebody must have told you. Heads it is. You win. We are quits, Doctor," said the Idiot.

"But I am still without the quarter," the physician observed.

"Yep," said the Idiot. "But there's one more way out of it. I'll buy the telegram from you—C.O.D."

"Done," said the Doctor, holding out the message. "Here's your goods."

"And there's your money," said the Idiot, tossing the quarter across the table. "If you want to buy this message back at any time within the next sixty days, Doctor, I'll give you the refusal of it without extra charge."

And he folded the paper up and put it away in his pocketbook.

"Do the banks really ask for so much security when they make a loan?" asked the Poet.

"Hear him, will you!" cried the Idiot. "There's your lucky man. He's never had to face a bank president in order to avoid the cold glances of the grocer. No cashier ever asked him how many times he had been sentenced to states-prison before he'd discount his note. Do they ask security? Security isn't the name for it. They demand a blockade, establish a quarantine. They require the would-be debtor to build up a wall as high as Chimborazo and as invulnerable as Gibraltar between them and the loss before they will part with a dime. Why, they wouldn't discount a note to his own order for Andrew Carnegie for seventeen cents without his indorsement. Do they ask security!"

"Well, I didn't know," said the Poet. "I never had anything to do with banks except as a small depositor in the savings-bank."

"Fortunate man," said the Idiot. "I wish I could say as much. I borrowed five hundred dollars once from a bank, and what the deuce do you suppose they did?"

"I don't know," said the Poet. "What?"

"They made me pay it back," said the Idiot, mournfully, "although I needed it just as much when it was due as when I borrowed it. The cashier was a friend of mine, too. But I got even with 'em. I refused to borrow another cent from their darned old institution. They lost my custom then and there. If it hadn't been for that inconsiderate act I should probably have gone on borrowing from them for years, and instead of owing them nothing to-day, as I do, I should have been their debtor to the tune of two or three thousand dollars."

"Don't you take any stock in what the Idiot tells you in that matter, Mr. Poet," said Mr. Brief. "The national banks are perfectly justified in protecting themselves as they do. If they didn't demand collateral security they'd be put out of business in fifteen minutes by people like the Idiot, who consider it a hardship to have to pay up."

"As the lady said when she was asked the name of her favorite author, 'Pshaw!'" retorted the Idiot. "Likewise fudge—a whole panful of fudges! I don't object to paying my debts; fact is, I know of no greater pleasure. What I do object to is the kind of collateral the banks demand. They always want something a man hasn't got and, in most cases, hasn't any chance of getting. If I had a thousand-dollar bond I wouldn't need to borrow five hundred dollars, yet when I go to the bank and ask for the five hundred the thousand-dollar bond is what they ask for."

"Not always," said Mr. Brief. "If you can get your note indorsed you can get the money."

"That's true enough, but fellows like myself can't always find a captain of industry who is willing to take a long-shot to do the indorsing," said the Idiot. "Besides, under the indorsement plan you merely ask another man to be responsible for your debt, and that isn't fair. The whole system is wrong. Every man to his own collateral, I say. Give me the bank that will lend money to the chap that needs it on the security of his own product. Mr. Whitechoker, say, is short on cash and long on sermons. My style of bank would take one barrel of his sermons and salt 'em down in the safe-deposit company as security for the money he needs. The Poet here, finding the summer approaching and not a cent in hand to replenish his wardrobe, should be able to secure an advance of two or three hundred dollars on his sonnets, rondeaux, and lyrics—one dollar for each two-and-a-half-dollar sonnet, and so on. The grocer should be able to borrow money on his dried apples, his vinegar pickles, his canned asparagus, and other non-perishable assets, such as dog-biscuit, Roquefort cheese, and California raisins. The tailor seeking an accommodation of five hundred dollars should not be asked how many times he has been sentenced to jail for arson, and required to pay in ten thousand shares of Steel common, in order to get his grip on the currency, but should be approached appropriately and asked how many pairs of trousers he is willing to pledge as security for the loan."

"I don't know where I would come in on that proposition," said the Doctor. "There are times when we physicians need money, too."

"Pooh!" said the Idiot. "You are not a non-producer. It doesn't take a very smart doctor these days to produce patients, does it? You could assign your cases to the bank. One little case of hypochondria alone ought to be a sufficient guarantee of a steady income for years, properly managed. If you haven't learned how to keep your patients in such shape that they have to send for you two or three times a week, you'd better go back to the medical school and fit yourself for your real work in life. You never knew a plumber to be so careless of his interests as to clean up a job all at once, and what the plumber is to the household, the physician should be to the individual. Same way with Mr. Brief. With the machinery of the law in its present shape there is absolutely no excuse for a lawyer who settles any case inside of fifteen years, by which time it is reasonable to suppose his client will get into some new trouble that will keep him going as a paying concern for fifteen more. There isn't a field of human endeavor in which a man applies himself industriously that does not produce something that should be a negotiable security."

"How about burglars?" queried the Bibliomaniac.

"I stand corrected," said the Idiot. "The burglar is an exception, but then he is an exception also at the banks. The expert burglar very seldom leaves any security for what he gets at the banks, and so he isn't affected by the situation one way or the other."

"Oh, well," said Mr. Brief, rising, "it's only a pipe-dream all the way through. They might start in on such a proposition, but it would never last. When you went in to borrow fifteen dollars, putting up your idiocy as collateral, the emptiness of the whole scheme would reveal itself."

"You never can tell," observed the Idiot. "Even under their present system the banks have done worse than that."

"Never!" cried the Lawyer.

"Yes, sir," replied the Idiot. "Only the other day I saw in the papers that a bank out in Oklahoma had loaned a man ten thousand dollars on sixty thousand shares of Hot Air preferred."

"And is that worse than Idiocy?" demanded Mr. Brief.

"Infinitely," said the Idiot. "If a bank lost fifteen dollars on my idiocy it would be out ninety-nine hundred and eighty-five dollars less than that Oklahoma institution is on its hot-air loan."

"Bosh! What's Hot Air worth on the Exchange to-day?"

"As a selling proposition, zero and commissions off," said the Idiot. "Fact is, they've changed its name. It is now known as International Nitting."

CHAPTER V

HE SUGGESTS A COMIC OPERA

"THERE'S a harvest for you," said the Idiot, as he perused a recently published criticism of a comic opera. "There have been thirty-nine new comic operas produced this year and four of 'em were worth seeing. It is very evident that the Gilbert and Sullivan industry hasn't gone to the wall whatever slumps other enterprises have suffered from."

"That is a goodly number," said the Poet. "Thirty-nine, eh? I knew there was a raft of them, but I had no idea there were as many as that."

"Why don't you go in and do one, Mr. Poet?" suggested the Idiot. "They tell me it's as easy as rolling off a log. All you've got to do is to forget all your ideas and remember all the old jokes you ever heard, slap 'em together around a lot of dances, write two dozen lyrics about some Googoo Belle, hire a composer, and there you are. Hanged if I haven't thought of writing one myself."

"I fancy it isn't as easy as it looks," observed the Poet. "It requires just as much thought to be thoughtless as it does to be thoughtful."

"Nonsense," said the Idiot. "I'd undertake the job cheerfully if some manager would make it worth my while, and, what's more, if I ever got into the swing of the business I'll bet I could turn out a libretto a day for three days of the week for the next two months."

"If I had your confidence I'd try it," laughed the Poet, "but, alas! in making me Nature did not design a confidence man."

"Nonsense, again," said the Idiot. "Any man who can get the editors to print sonnets to 'Diana's Eyebrow,' and little lyrics of Madison Square, Longacre Square, Battery Place, and Boston Common, the way you do, has a right to consider himself an adept at bunco. I tell you what I'll do with you: I'll swap off my confidence for your lyrical facility, and see what I can do. Why can't we collaborate and get up a libretto for next season? They tell me there's large money in it."

"There certainly is if you catch on," said the Poet. "Vastly more than in any other kind of writing that I know. I don't know but that I would like to collaborate with you on something of the sort. What is your idea?"

"Mind's a blank on the subject," sighed the Idiot. "That's the reason I think I can turn the trick. As I said before, you don't need ideas. Better go without 'em. Just sit down and write."

"But you must have some kind of a story," persisted the Poet.

"Not to begin with," said the Idiot. "Just write your choruses and songs, slap in your jokes, fasten 'em together, and the thing is done. First act, get your hero and heroine into trouble. Second act, get 'em out."

"And for the third?" queried the Poet.

"Don't have a third," said the Idiot. "A third is always superfluous; but, if you must have it, make up some kind of a vaudeville show and stick it in between the first and second."

"Tush!" said the Bibliomaniac. "That would make a gay comic opera."

"Of course it would, Mr. Bib," the Idiot agreed. "And that's what we want. If there's anything in this world that I hate more than another it is a sombre comic opera. I've been to a lot of 'em, and I give you my word of honor that next to a funeral a comic opera that lacks gayety is one of the most depressing functions known to modern science. Some of 'em are enough to make an undertaker weep with jealous rage. I went to one of 'em last week called 'The Skylark,' with an old chum of mine who is a surgeon. You can imagine what sort of a thing it was when I tell you that after the first act he suggested we leave the theatre and come back here and have some fun cutting my leg off. He vowed that if he ever went to another opera by the same people he'd take ether beforehand."

"I shouldn't think that would be necessary," sneered the Bibliomaniac. "If it was as bad as all that, why didn't it put you to sleep?"

"It did," said the Idiot. "But the music kept waking us up again. There was no escape from it except that of actual physical flight."

"Well, about this collaboration of ours," suggested the Poet. "What do you think we should do first?"

"Write an opening chorus, of course," said the Idiot. "What did you suppose? A finale? Something like this:

"If you want to know who we are,
Just ask the Evening Star,
*   As he smiles on high*
*   In the deep-blue sky,*
With his tralala-la-la-la.
We are maidens sweet
With tripping feet,
And the googoo eyes
Of the skippity-hi's,
And the smile of the fair gazoo;
And you'll find our names
'Mongst the wondrous dames
Of the Who's Who-hoo-hoo-hoo."

"Get that sung with spirit by sixty-five ladies with blond wigs and gold slippers, otherwise dressed up in the uniform of a troop of Russian cavalry, and you've got your venture launched."

"Where can you find people like that?" asked the Bibliomaniac.

"New York's full of 'em," replied the Idiot.

"I don't mean the people to act that sort of thing—but where would you lay your scene?" explained the Bibliomaniac.

"Oh, any old place in the Pacific Ocean," said the Idiot. "Make your own geography—everybody else does. There's a million islands out there of one kind or another, and as defenceless as a two-weeks'-old infant. If you want a real one, fish it out and fire ahead. If you don't, make one up for yourself and call it 'The Isle of Piccolo,' or something of that sort. After you've got your chorus going, introduce your villain, who should be a man with a deep bass voice and a piratical past. He's the chap who rules the roost and is going to marry the heroine to-morrow. That will make a bully song:

> *"I'm a pirate bold*
> *With a heart so cold*
> *That it turns the biggest joys to solemn sorrow;*
> *And the hero-ine,*
> *With her eyes so fine,*
> *I am going to—marry—to-morrow.*

CHORUS

> *"He is go-ing to-marry—to-morrow*
> *The maid with a heart full of sorrow;*
> *For her we are sorry*
> *For she weds to-morry—*
> *She is going to-marry—to-morrow. "*

"Gee!" added the Idiot, enthusiastically, "can't you almost hear that already?"

"I am sorry to say," said Mr. Brief, "that I can. You ought to call your heroine Drivelina."

"Splendid!" cried the Idiot. "Drivelina goes. Well, then, on comes Drivelina, and this beast of a pirate grabs her by the hand and makes love to her as if he thought wooing was a game of snap-the-whip. She sings a soprano solo of protest, and the pirate summons his hirelings to cast Drivelina into a Donjuan cell, when boom! an American war-ship appears on the horizon. The crew, under the leadership of a man with a squeaky tenor voice, named Lieutenant Somebody or Other, comes ashore, puts Drivelina under the protection of the American flag, while his crew sing the following:

> *"We are jackies, jackies, jackies,*
> *And we smoke the best tobaccys*
> > *You can find from Zanzibar to Honeyloo.*
> *And we fight for Uncle Sammy,*
> *Yes, indeed we do, for damme*
> > *You can bet your life that that's the thing to do,*
> > > *Doodle-do!*
> > *You can bet your life that that's the thing to doodle—*
> > > *doodle—doodle—doodle-do."*

"Eh! What?" demanded the Idiot.

"Well—what yourself?" asked the Lawyer. "This is your job. What next?"

"Well—the pirate gets lively, tries to assassinate the lieutenant, who kills half the natives with his sword, and is about to slay the pirate when he discovers that he is his long-lost father," said the Idiot. "The heroine then sings a pathetic love-song about her baboon baby, in a green light to the accompaniment of a lot of pink satin monkeys banging cocoanut-shells together. This drowsy lullaby puts the lieutenant and his forces to sleep, and the curtain falls on their capture by the pirate and his followers, with the chorus singing:

> *"Hooray for the pirate bold,*
> *With his pockets full of gold;*
> > *He's going to marry to-morrow.*
> > *To-morrow he'll marry,*
> > *Yes, by the Lord Harry,*
> *He's go-ing—to-marry—to-mor-row!*
> *And that's a thing to doodle—doodle-doo."*

"There," said the Idiot, after a pause. "How is that for a first act?"

"It's about as lucid as most of them," said the Poet, "but, after all, you have got a story there, and you said you didn't need one."

"I said you didn't need one to start with," corrected the Idiot. "And I've proved it. I didn't have that story in mind when I started. That's where the easiness of the thing comes in. Why, I didn't even have to think of a name for the heroine. The inspiration for that popped right out of Mr. Brief's mouth as smoothly as though the name Drivelina had been

written on his heart for centuries. Then the title—'The Isle of Piccolo'—
that's a dandy, and I give you my word of honor, I'd never even thought
of a title for the opera until that revealed itself like a flash from the blue;
and as for the coon song, 'My Baboon Baby,' there's a chance there for
a Zanzibar act that will simply make Richard Wagner and Reginald de
Koven writhe with jealousy. Can't you imagine the lilt of it:

> *"My bab-boon—ba-habee,*
> *My bab-boon—ba-habee—*
> *I love you dee-her-lee*
> *Yes dee-hee-hee-er-lee.*
> *My baboon—ba-ha-bee,*
> *My baboon—ba-ha-bee,*
> *My baboon—ba-hay-hay-hay-hay-hay-hay-bee-bee."*

"And all those pink satin monkeys bumping their cocoanut-shells
together in the green moonlight—"

"Well, after the first act, what?" asked the Bibliomaniac.

"The usual intermission," said the Idiot. "You don't have to write
that. The audience generally knows what to do."

"But your second act?" asked the Poet.

"Oh, come off," said the Idiot, rising. "We were to do this thing in
collaboration. So far, I've done the whole blooming business. I'll leave
the second act to you. When you collaborate, Mr. Poet, you've got to do
a little colabbing on your own account. What did you think you were to
do—collect the royalties?"

"I'm told," said the Lawyer, "that that is sometimes the hardest thing
to do in a comic opera."

"Well, I'll be self-sacrificing," said the Idiot, "and bear my full share
of it."

"It seems to me," said the Bibliomaniac, "that that opera produced in
the right place might stand a chance of a run."

"Thank you," said the Idiot. "After all, Mr. Bib, you are a man of
some penetration. How long a run?"

"One consecutive night," said the Bibliomaniac.

"Ah—and where?" demanded the Idiot, with a smile.

"At Bloomingdale," answered the Bibliomaniac, severely.

"That's a very good idea," said the Idiot. "When you go back there,
Mr. Bib, I wish you'd suggest it to the superintendent."

CHAPTER VI

HE DISCUSSES FAME

MR. POET," said the Idiot, the other morning as his friend, the Rhymster, took his place beside him at the breakfast-table, "tell me: How long have you been writing poetry?"

"Oh, I don't know," said the Poet, modestly. "I don't know that I've ever written any. I've turned out a lot of rhymes in my day, and have managed to make a fair living with them, but poetry is a different thing. The divine afflatus doesn't come to every one, you know; and I doubt if anybody will be able to say whether my work has shown an occasional touch of inspiration, or not until I have been dead fifty or a hundred years."

"Tut!" exclaimed the Idiot. "That's all nonsense. I am able to say now whether or not your work shows the occasional touch of inspiration. It does. In fact, it shows more than that. It shows a semi-occasional touch of inspiration. How long have you been in the business?"

"Eighteen years," sighed the Poet. "I began when I was twelve with a limerick. As I remember the thing, it went like this:

> *"There was a young man of Cohasset*
> *Turned on the red-hot water-faucet.*
> *When asked: 'Is it hot?'*
> *He answered, 'Well, thot*
> *Is a pretty mild way for to class it.'"*

"Good!" said the Idiot. "That wasn't a bad beginning for a boy of twelve."

"So my family thought," said the Poet. "My mother sent it to the Under the Evening Lamp Department of our town paper, and three weeks later I was launched. I've had the cacœthes scribendi ever since—but, alas! I got more fame in that brief hour of success than I have ever been able to win since. It is a mighty hard job, Mr. Idiot, making a name for yourself these days."

"That's the point I was getting at," said the Idiot, "and I wanted to have a talk with you on the subject. I've read a lot of your stuff in the past eight or ten years, and, in my humble judgment, it is better than any of that rhymed nonsense of Henry Wintergreen Boggs, whose name appears in the newspapers every day in the year; of Susan Aldershot Spinks, whose portrait is almost as common an occurrence in the papers as that of Lydia

Squinkham; of Circumflex Jones, the eminent sweet-singer of Arizona; or of Henderson Hartley MacFadd, the Canadian Browning, of whom the world is constantly hearing so much. I have wondered if you were going about it in the right way. What is your plan for winning fame?"

"Oh, I keep plodding away, doing the best I can all the while," said the Poet. "If there's any good in my stuff, or any stuff in my goods, I'll get my reward some day."

"Fifty or a hundred years after you're dead, eh?" said the Idiot.

"Yes," smiled the Poet.

"Well—your board-bills won't be high then, anyhow," said the Idiot. "That's one satisfaction, I presume. They tell me Homer hasn't eaten a thing for over twenty centuries. Seems to me, though, that if I were a poet I'd go in for a little fame while I was alive. It's all very nice to work the skin off your knuckles, and to twist your gray matter inside out until it crocks and fades, so that your great-grandchildren can swell around the country sporting a name that has become a household word, but I'm blessed if I care for that sort of thing. I don't believe in storing up caramels for some twenty-first-century baby that bears my name to cut his teeth on, when I have a sweet tooth of my own that is pining away for the lack of nourishment; and, if I were you, I'd go in for the new method. What if Browning and Tennyson and Longfellow and Poe did have to labor for years to win the laurel crown, that's no reason why you should do it. You might just as well reason that because your forefathers went from one city to another in a stage-coach you should eschew railways."

"I quite agree with you," replied the Poet. "But in literature there is no royal road to fame that I know of."

"What!" cried the Idiot. "No royal road to fame in letters! Why, where have you been living all these years, Mr. Poet? This is the age of the Get Fame-Quick Scheme. You can make a reputation in five minutes, if you only know the ropes. I know of at least two department stores where you can go and buy all you want of it, and in all its grades—from notoriety down to the straight goods."

"Fame? At a department store!" put in Mr. Whitechoker, incredulously.

"Certainly," said the Idiot. "Ready-made laurels on demand. Why not? It's the easiest thing in the world. Fact is, between you and me, I am considering a plan now for the promoting of a corporation to be called the United States Fame Company, Limited, the main purpose of which shall be to earn money for its stockholders by making its customers famous at so much per head. It won't make any difference whether the customer wishes to be famous as an actor, a novelist, or a poet, or any other old thing. We'll turn the trick for him, and guarantee him more than a taste of immortality."

"You may put me down for four dollars' worth of notoriety," said Mr. Brief, with a laugh.

"All right," said the Idiot, dryly. "There's a lot in your profession who like the cheap sort. But I warn you in advance that if you go in for cheap notoriety, you'll find it a pretty hard job getting anybody to sell you any eighteen-karat distinction later."

"Well," said the Poet, "I don't know that I can promise to be one of your customers until I know something of the quality of the fame you have to sell. Tell me of somebody you've made a name for, and I'll take the matter into consideration if I like the style of laurel you have placed on his brow."

"Lean over here and I'll whisper," said the Idiot. "I don't mind telling you, but I don't believe in giving away the secrets of the trade to the rest of these gentlemen."

The Poet did as he was bade, and the Idiot whispered a certain great name in his ear.

"No!" cried the Poet, incredulously.

"Yes, sir. Fact!" said the Idiot. "He was made famous in a night. The first thing we did was to get him to elongate his signature. He was writing as—P. K. Dubbins we'll call him, for the sake of the argument. Now a name like that couldn't be made great under any circumstances whatsoever, so we made him write it out in full: Philander Kenilworth Dubbins—regular broadside, you see. P. K. Dubbins was a pop-shot, but Philander Kenilworth Dubbins spreads out like a dum-dum bullet or hits you like a blast from a Gatling gun. Printed, it takes up a whole line of a newspaper column; put at the top of an advertisement, it strikes the eye with the convincing force of a circus-poster. You can't help seeing it, and it makes, when spoken, a mouthful that is nothing short of impressive and sonorous."

"Still," suggested Mr. Brief, with a wink at the Bibliomaniac, "you have only multiplied your difficulties by three. If it was hard for your friend Dubbins to make one name famous, I can't see that he improves matters by trying to make three names famous."

"On the modern business principle that to accomplish anything you must work on a large scale," said the Idiot. "Philander Kenilworth Dubbins was a better proposition than P. K. Dubbins. The difference between them in the mere matter of potentialities is the difference be-tween a corner grocery and a department store, or a kite with a tail and one without. Well, having created the name, the next thing to do was to exploit it, and we advertised Dubbins for all there was in him. We got

Mr. William Jones Brickbat, the eminent novelist, to say that he had read Dubbins's poems, and had not yet died; we got Edward Pinkham, the author of "The Man with the Watering-pot," to send us a type-written letter, saying that Dubbins was a coming man, and that his latest book, *Howls from Helicon*, contained many inspired lines. But, best of all, we prevailed upon the manufacturers of celluloid soap to print a testimonial from Dubbins himself, saying that there was no other soap like it in the market. That brought his name prominently before every magazine-reader in the country, because the celluloid-soap people are among the biggest advertisers of the day, and everywhere that soap ad went, why, Dubbins's testimonial went also, as faithfully as Mary's Little Lamb. After that we paid a shirt-making concern down-town to put out a new collar called "The Helicon," which they advertised widely with a picture of Dubbins's head sticking up out of the middle of it; and, finally, as a crowning achievement, we leased Dubbins for a year to a five-cent cigar company, who have placarded the fences, barns, and chicken-coops from Maine to California with the name of Dubbins—'Flora Dubbins: The Best Five-Cent Smoke in the Market.'"

"And thus you made the name of Dubbins famous in letters!" sneered the Doctor.

"That was only the preliminary canter," replied the Idiot. "So far, Dubbins's greatness was confined to fences, barns, chicken-coops, and the advertising columns of the magazines. The next thing was to get him written up in the newspapers. That sort of thing can't be bought, but you can acquire it by subtlety. Plan one was to make an after-dinner speaker out of Dubbins. This was easy. There are a million public dinners every year, but a limited supply of good speakers; so, with a little effort, we got Dubbins on five toast-cards, hired a humorist out in Wisconsin to write five breezy speeches for him, Dubbins committed them to memory, and they went off like hot-cakes. Morning papers would come out with Dubbins's picture printed in between that of Bishop Potter and a member of the cabinet, who also spoke. Copies of Dubbins's speeches were handed to the reporters before the dinner began, so that it didn't make any difference whether Dubbins spoke them or not—the papers had 'em next morning just the same, and inside of six months you couldn't read an account of any public banquet without running up against the name of Philander Kenilworth Dubbins."

"Well, I declare!" ejaculated Mr. Whitechoker. "What a strange affair!"

"Then we got Dubbins's publishers to take a hand," said the Idiot. "They issued a monthly budget of gossip concerning their authors, which newspaper editors all over quoted in their interesting items of the day.

From these paragraphs the public learned that Dubbins wrote between 4 A.M. and breakfast-time; that Dubbins never penned a line without having a tame rabbit, named Romola, sitting alongside of his ink-pot; that Dubbins got his ideas for his wonderful poem, 'The Mystery of Life,' from hearing a canary inadvertently whistle a bar of 'Hiawatha;' that Dubbins was the best-dressed author in the State of New York, affecting green plaid waistcoats, pink shirts, and red neckties; witty things that Dubbins's boy had said about Dubbins's work to Dubbins himself were also spread all over the land, until finally Philander Kenilworth Dubbins became a select series of household words in every town, city, and hamlet in the United States. And there he is to-day—a great man, bearing a great name, made for him by his friends. *Howls from Helicon* is full of bad poems, but Dubbins is a son of Parnassus just the same. Now we propose to do it for others. For five dollars down, Mr. Poet, I'll make you conspicuous; for ten, I'll make you notorious; for fifty, I'll make you famous; for a hundred, I'll give you immortality."

"Good!" cried the Poet. "Immortality for a hundred dollars is cheap. I'll take that."

"You will?" said the Idiot, joyfully. "Put up your money."

"All right," laughed the Poet. "I'll pay—C. O. D."

"Another hundred gone!" moaned the Idiot, as the party broke up and its members went their several ways. "I think it's abominable that this commercial spirit of the age should have affected even you poets. You ought to have gone into business, old man, and left the Muses alone. You've got too good a head for poetry."

CHAPTER VII

ON THE DECADENCE OF APRIL-FOOL'S-DAY

"I AM sorry to observe," said the Idiot, as he sat down at the breakfast-table yesterday morning, "that the good old customs of my youthful days are dying out by slow degrees, and the celebrations that once filled my childish soul with glee are no longer a part of the pleasures of the young. Actually, Mr. Whitechoker, I got through the whole day yesterday without sitting on a single pin or smashing my toes against a brickbat hid beneath a hat. What on earth can be coming over the boys of the land that they no longer avail themselves of the privileges of the fool-tide?"

"Fool-tide's good," said Mr. Brief. "Where did you get that?"

"Oh, I pried it out of my gray-matter 'way back in the last century," said the Idiot. "It grew out of a simple little prank I played one April 1st upon an uncle of mine. I bored a hole in the middle of a pine log and filled it with powder. We had it that night on the hearth, and a moment later there wasn't any hearth. In talking the matter over later with my father and mother and the old gentleman, in order to turn the discussion into more genial channels, I asked why, if the Yule-log was appropriate for the Yule-tide, the Fool-log wasn't appropriate for the Fool-tide."

"I hope you got the answer you deserved," said the Bibliomaniac.

"I did," sighed the Idiot. "I got all there was coming to me—slippers, trunk-strap, hair-brush, and plain hand; but it was worth it. All the glories of Vesuvius, Etna, Popocatepetl, and Pelée rolled into one could never thereafter induce in me anything approaching that joyous sensation that I derived from the spectacle of that fool-log and that happy hearth soaring up through the chimney together, hand in hand, and taking with them such portions of the flues, andirons, and other articles of fireplace vertu as cared to join them in their upward flight."

"You must have been a holy terror as a boy," said the Doctor. "I should not have cared to live on your block."

"Oh, I wasn't so bad," observed the Idiot. "I never was vicious or malicious in what I did. If I poured vitriol into the coffee-pot at breakfast my father and mother knew that I didn't do it to give pain to anybody. If I hid under my maiden aunt's bed and barked like a bull-dog after she had retired, dear old Tabitha knew that it was all done in a spirit of pleasantry. When I glued my grandfather's new teeth together with stratina, that splendid old man was perfectly aware that I had no grudge I was trying thus to repay; and certainly the French teacher at school, when he sat down on an iron bear-trap I had set for him in his chair, never entertained the notion that there was the slightest animosity in my act."

"By jingo!" cried the Bibliomaniac. "I'd have spanked you good and hard if I'd been your mother."

"Don't you fret—she did it; that is, she did up to the time I was ten years old, and then she had such a shock she gave up corporeal punishment altogether," said the Idiot.

"Had a shock, eh?" smiled the Lawyer. "Nearly killed you, I suppose, giving you what you deserved?"

"No," said the Idiot. "Spanked me with a hair-brush without having removed a couple of Excelsior torpedoes from my pistol-pocket. On the second whack I appeared to explode. Poor woman! She didn't know I was loaded, and from that time on she was as afraid of me as most other women are of a gun."

"I'd have turned you over to your father," said the Bibliomaniac, indignantly.

"She did," said the Idiot, sadly. "I never used explosives again. In later years I took up the milder April-fool diversions, such as filling the mucilage-pot with ink and the ink-pot with mucilage; mixing the granulated sugar with white sand; putting powdered brick into the red-pepper pot; inserting kerosene-oil into the sweet-oil bottle, and little things like that. I squandered a whole dollar one April-fool's-day sending telegrams to my uncles and aunts, telling them to come and dine with us that night; and they all came, too, although my father and mother were dining out that evening, and—oh dear, April-fool's-day is not what it used to be. The boys and girls of the present generation are little old men and women with no pranks left in them. Why, I don't believe that nine out of ten boys, who are about to enter college this spring, could rig up a successful tick-tack on a window to save their lives; and the joy of carrying a piece of twine across the sidewalk from a front-door knob to a lamp-post, hat-high, and then sitting back in the seclusion of a convenient area and watching the plug-hats of the people go down before it—that is a joy that seems to be wholly untasted of the present generation of infantile dignitaries that we call the youth of the land. What is the matter with 'em, do you suppose?"

"I guess we're getting civilized," said Mr. Brief. "That seems to me to be the most likely explanation of this deplorable situation, as you appear to think it. For my part, I'm glad if what you say is true. Of all rotten things in the world the practical jokes of April-fool's-day bear away the palm. There was a time, ten years ago, when I hardly dared eat anything on the first of April. I was afraid to find my coffee made of ink, my muffin stuffed with cotton, cod-liver oil in my salad-dressing, and mayonnaise in my cream-puffs. Such tricks are the tricks of barbarians, and I shall rejoice when April 1st as a day of special privilege for idiots and savages has been removed from the calendar."

"I am afraid," said Mr. Whitechoker, "that I, too, must join the ranks of those who rejoice if the old-time customs of the day are now honored more in the breach than in the observance. Ever since that unhappy Sunday morning some years ago when somebody substituted a breakfast bill-of-fare for the card containing the notes for my sermon, I have mistrusted the humor of the April-fool joke. Instead of my text, as I glanced at what I supposed was my note-card, my eyes fell upon the statement that fruit taken from the table would be charged for; instead of my firstly, secondly, thirdly, and fourthly, my eyes were confronted by Fish, Eggs, Hot Bread, and To Order. And, finally, in place of the key-line of my peroration, what should obtrude itself upon my vision but that coarse and vulgar legend: Corkage, one dollar. I never found out who did it, and, as a Christian man, I hope I never shall, for I should much deprecate the spirit of animosity with which I should inevitably regard the person who had so offended."

"I'll bet you preached a bully good sermon, allee samee," said the Idiot.

"Well," smiled Mr. Whitechoker, "the congregation did seem to think that it held more fire than usual; but I can assure you, my young friend, it was more the fire of external wrath than of an inward spiritual grace."

"Well," said the Bibliomaniac, "we ought to be thankful the old tricks are going out. As Mr. Brief suggests, we are beginning to be civilized—"

"I don't think it's civilization," said the Idiot. "I think the kids are just discouraged, that's all. They're clever, these youngsters, but when it comes to putting up games, they're not in it with their far more foxy fathers. What's the use of playing April-fool jokes on your daddy, when your daddy is playing April-fool jokes on the public all the year round? That's the way they reason. No son of George W. Midas, the financier, is going to get any satisfaction out of handing his father a loaded cigar, when he knows that the old man is handling that sort of thing every day in his business as a promoter of the United States Hot Air Company. What fun is there in giving your sister a caramel filled with tabasco-sauce when you can watch your father selling eleven dollars' worth of Amalgamated Licorice stock to the dear public for forty-seven fifty? The gum-drop filled with cotton loses its charm when you contrast it with Consolidated Radium containing one part of radium and ninety-nine parts of water. Who cares to hide a clay brick under a hat for somebody to kick, when there are concerns in palatial offices all over town selling gold bricks to a public that doesn't seem to have any kick left in it? I tell you it has discouraged the kid to see to what scientific heights the April-fool industry has been developed, and as a result he has abandoned the field. He knows he can't compete."

"That's all right as an explanation of the youngster whose parent is engaged in that sort of business," said the Doctor. "But there are others."

"True," said the Idiot. "The others stay out of it out of sheer pity. When they are tempted to sew up the legs of their daddy's trousers in order to fitly celebrate the day, or to fill his collar-box with collars five sizes too small for him, they say, 'No. Let us refrain. The governor has had trouble enough with his International Yukon Anticipated Brass shares this year. He's had all the fooling he can stand. We will give the old gentleman a rest!' Fact is, come to look at it, the decadence of April 1st as a day of foolery for the young is no mystery, after all. The youngsters are not more civilized than we used to be, but they have had the intelligence to perceive the exact truth of the situation."

"Which is?" asked Mr. Brief.

"That the ancient art of practical joking has become a business. April-fool's-day has been incorporated by the leading financiers of the age, and is doing a profitable trade all over the world all the year round. Private enterprise is simply unable to compete."

"I am rather surprised, nevertheless," said Mr. Brief, "that you yourself have abandoned the field. You are just the sort of person who would keep on in that kind of thing, despite the discouragements."

"Oh, I haven't abandoned the field," said the Idiot. "I did play an April-fool joke last Friday."

"What was that?" asked Mr. Whitechoker, interested.

"I told Mrs. Pedagog that I would pay my bill to-morrow," replied the Idiot, as he rose from the table and left the room.

CHAPTER VIII

SPRING AND ITS POETRY

"WELL, Mr. Idiot," said Mrs. Pedagog, genially, as the Idiot entered the breakfast-room, "what can I do for you this fine spring morning? Will you have tea or coffee?"

"I think I'd like a cup of boiled iron, with two lumps of quinine and a spoonful of condensed nerve-milk in it," replied the Idiot, wearily. "Somehow or other I have managed to mislay my spine this morning. Ethereal mildness has taken the place of my backbone."

"Those tired feelings, eh?" said Mr. Brief.

"Yeppy," replied the Idiot. "Regular thing with me. Every year along about the middle of April I have to fasten a poker on my back with straps, in order to stand up straight; and as for my knees—well, I never know where they are in the merry, merry spring-time. I'm quite sure that if I didn't wear brass caps on them my legs would bend backward. I wonder if this neighborhood is malarious."

"Not in the slightest degree," observed the Doctor. "This is the healthiest neighborhood in town. The trouble with you is that you have a swampy mind, and it is the miasmatic oozings of your intellect that reduce you to the condition of physical flabbiness of which you complain. You might swallow the United States Steel Trust, and it wouldn't help you a bit, and ten thousand bottles of nerve-milk, or any other tonic known to science, would be powerless to reach the seat of your disorder. What you need to stiffen you up is a pair of those armored trousers the Crusaders used to wear in the days of chivalry, to bolster up your legs, and a strait-jacket to keep your back up."

"Thank you, kindly," said the Idiot. "If you'll give me a prescription, which I can have made up at your tailor's, I'll have it filled, unless you'll add to my ever-increasing obligation to you by lending me your own strait-jacket. I promise to keep it straight and to return it the moment you feel one of your fits coming on."

The Doctor's response was merely a scornful gesture, and the Idiot went on:

"It's always seemed a very queer thing to me that this season of the year should be so popular with everybody," he said. "To me it's the mushiest of times. Mushy bones; mushy poetry; mush for breakfast, fried, stewed, and boiled. The roads are mushy; lovers thaw out and get mushier than ever.

"In the spring the blasts of winter all are stilled in solemn hush.
In the spring the young man's fancy lightly turns to thoughts of
mush.
In the spring—"

"You ought to be ashamed of yourself to trifle with so beautiful a poem," interrupted the Bibliomaniac, indignantly.

"Who's trifling with a beautiful poem?" demanded the Idiot.

"You are—'Locksley Hall'—and you know it," retorted the Bibliomaniac.

"Locksley nothing," said the Idiot. "What I was reciting is not from 'Locksley Hall' at all. It's a little thing of my own that I wrote six years ago called 'Spring Unsprung.' It may not contain much delicate sentiment, but it's got more solid information in it of a valuable kind than you'll find in ten 'Locksley Halls' or a dozen Etiquette Columns in the *Lady's Away From Home Magazine*. It has saved a lot of people from pneumonia and other disorders of early spring, I am quite certain, and the only person I ever heard criticise it unfavorably was a doctor I know who said it spoiled his business."

"I should admire to hear it," said the Poet. "Can't you let us have it?"

"Certainly," replied the Idiot. "It goes on like this:

"In the spring I'll take you driving, take you driving, Maudy
dear,
But I beg of you be careful at this season of the year.
It is true the birds are singing, singing sweetly all their notes,
But you'll later find them wearing canton-flannel 'round their
throats.
It is true the lark doth warble, 'Spring is here,' with bird-like fire,
'All is warmth and all is genial,' but I fear the lark's a liar.
All is warmth for fifteen minutes, that is true; but wait awhile,
And you'll find that April's weather has not ever changed its
style;
And beware of April's weather, it is pleasant for a spell,
But, like little Johnny's future, you can't always sometimes tell.
Often modest little violets, peeping up from out their beds
In the balmy morn by night-time have bad colds within their
heads;
And the buttercup and daisy twinkling gayly on the lawn,
Sing by night a different story from their carollings at dawn;
And the blossoms of the morning, hailing spring with joyous
frenzy,

When the twilight falls upon them often droop with influenzy.
So, dear Maudy, when we're driving, put your linen duster on,
And your lovely Easter bonnet, if you wish to, you may don;
But be careful to have with you sundry garments warm and thick:
Woollen gloves, a muff, and ear-tabs, from the ice-box get the
 pick;
There's no telling what may happen ere we've driven twenty
 miles,
April flirts with chill December, and is full of other wiles.
Bring your parasol, O Maudy—it is good for tête-à-têtes;
At the same time you would better also bring your hockey skates.
There's no telling from the noon-tide, with the sun a-shining
 bright,
Just what kind of winter weather we'll be up against by night."

"Referring to the advice," said Mr. Brief, "that's good. I don't think much of the poetry."

"There was a lot more of it," said the Idiot, "but it escapes me at the moment. Four lines I do remember, however:

"Pin no faith to weather prophets—all their prophecies are fakes,
Roulette-wheels are plain and simple to the notions April takes.
Keep your children in the nursery—never mind it if they pout—
And, above all, do not let your furnace take an evening out."

"Well," said the Poet, "if you're going to the poets for advice, I presume your rhymes are all right. But I don't think it is the mission of the poet to teach people common-sense."

"That's the trouble with the whole tribe of poets," said the Idiot. "They think they are licensed to do and say all sorts of things that other people can't do and say. In a way I agree with you that a poem shouldn't necessarily be a treatise on etiquette or a sequence of health hints, but it should avoid misleading its readers. Take that fellow who wrote

"'Sweet primrose time! When thou art here
 I go by grassy ledges
Of long lane-side, and pasture mead,
 And moss-entangled hedges.'

That's very lovely, and, as far as it goes, it is all right. There's no harm in doing what the poet so delicately suggests, but I think there should have been other stanzas for the protection of the reader like this:

"But have a care, oh, readers fair,
To take your mackintoshes,
And on your feet be sure to wear
A pair of stanch galoshes.

"Nor should you fail when seeking out
The primrose, golden yeller,
To have at hand somewhere about
A competent umbrella.

Thousands of people are inspired by lines like the original to go gallivanting all over the country in primrose time, to return at dewy eve with all the incipient symptoms of pneumonia. Then there's the case of Wordsworth. He was one of the loveliest of the Nature poets, but he's eternally advising people to go out in the early spring and lie on the grass somewhere, listening to cuckoos doing their cooking, watching the daffodils at their daily dill, and hearing the crocus cuss; and some sentimental reader out in New Jersey thinks that if Wordsworth could do that sort of thing, and live to be eighty years old, there's no reason why he shouldn't do the same thing. What's the result? He lies on the grass for two hours and suffers from rheumatism for the next ten years."

"Tut!" said the Poet. "I am surprised at you. You can't blame Wordsworth because some New Jerseyman makes a jackass of himself."

"In a way all writers should be responsible for the effect of what they write on their readers," said the Idiot. "When a poet of Wordsworth's eminence, directly or indirectly, advises people to go out and lie on the grass in early spring, he owes it to his public to caution them that in some localities it is not a good thing to do. A rhymed foot-note—

"This habit, by-the-way, is good
In climes south of the Mersey;
But, I would have it understood,
It's risky in New Jersey—

would fulfil all the requirements of the special individual to whom I have referred, and would have shown that the poet himself was ever mindful of the welfare of his readers."

The Poet was apparently unconvinced, so the Idiot continued:

"Mind you, old man, I think all this poetry is beautiful," he said; "but you poets are too prone to confine your attention to the pleasant aspects of the season. Here, for instance, is a poet who asks

'What are the dearest treasures of spring?'

and then goes on to name the cheapest as an answer to his question. The primrose, the daffodil, the rosy haze that veils the forest bare, the sparkle of the myriad-dimpled sea, a kissing-match between the sunbeams and the rain-drops, reluctant hopes, the twitter of swallows on the wing, and all that sort of thing. You'd think spring was an iridescent dream of ecstatic things; but of the tired feeling that comes over you, the spine of jelly, the wabbling knee, the chills and fever that come from sniffing 'the scented breath of dewy April's eve,' the doctor's bills, and such like things are never mentioned. It isn't fair. It's all right to tell about the other things, but don't forget the drawbacks. If I were writing that poem I'd have at least two stanzas like this:

> *"And other dearest treasures of spring*
> *Are daily draughts of withering, blithering squills,*
> *To cure my aching bones of darksome chills;*
> *And at the door my loved physician's ring;*

> *"The tender sneezes of the early day;*
> *The sudden drop of Mr. Mercury;*
> *The veering winds from S. to N. by E.—*
> *And hunting flats to move to in the May.*

You see, that makes not only a more comprehensive picture, but does not mislead anybody into the belief the spring is all velvet, which it isn't by any means."

"Oh, bosh!" cried the Poet, very much nettled, as he rose from the table. "I suppose if you had your way you'd have all poetry submitted first to a censor, the way they do with plays in London."

"No, I wouldn't have a censor; he'd only increase taxes unnecessarily," said the Idiot, folding up his napkin, and also rising to leave. "I'd just let the Board of Health pass on them; it isn't a question of morals so much as of sanitation."

CHAPTER IX

ON FLAT-HUNTING

"AHA!" cried the Poet, briskly rubbing his hands together, and drawing a deep breath of satisfaction, "these be great days for people who are fond of the chase, who love the open, and who would commune with Nature in her most lovely mood. Just look out of that window, Mr. Idiot, and drink in the joyous sunshine. Egad! sir, even the asphalted pavement and the brick-and-mortar façade of the houses opposite, bathed in that golden light, seem glorified."

"Thanks," said the Idiot, wearily, "but I guess I won't. I'm afraid that while I was drinking in those glorified flats opposite and digesting the golden-mellow asphalt, you would fasten that poetic grip of yours upon my share of the blossoming buckwheats. Furthermore, I've been enjoying the chase for two weeks now, and, to tell you the honest truth, I am long on it. There is such a thing as chasing too much, so if you don't mind I'll sublet my part of the contract for gazing out of the window at gilt-edged Nature as she appears in the city to you. Mary, move Mr. Poet's chair over to the window so that he may drink in the sunshine comfortably, and pass his share of the sausages to me."

"What have you been chasing, Mr. Idiot?" asked the Doctor. "Birds or the fast-flitting dollar?"

"Flats," said the Idiot.

"I didn't know you Wall Street people needed to hunt flats," said the Bibliomaniac. "I thought they just walked into your offices and presented themselves for skinning."

"I don't mean the flats we live on," explained the Idiot. "It's the flats we live in that I have been after."

The landlady looked up inquiringly. Mr. Idiot's announcement sounded ominous.

"To my mind, flat-hunting," the Idiot continued, "is one of the most interesting branches of sport. It involves quite as much uncertainty as the pursuit of the whirring partridge; your game is quite as difficult to lure as the speckled trout darting hither and yon in the grassy pool; it involves no shedding of innocent blood, as in the case of a ride across-country with a pack in full pursuit of the fox; and strikes me as possessing greater dignity than running forty miles through the cabbage-patches of Long Island in search of a bag of ainse seed. When the sporting instinct arises in my soul and reaches that full-tide where nothing short of action will hold it in control, I never think of starting for Maine to shoot the festive moose, nor do I squander my limited resources on a foggy hunt for the elusive canvasback in the Maryland marshes. I just go to the nearest cab-stand, strike a bargain with Mr. Jehu for an afternoon's use of his hansom, and go around the town hunting flats. It requires very little previous preparation; it involves no prolonged absences from home; you do not need rubber boots unless you propose to investigate the cellars or intend to go far afield into the suburban boroughs of this great city; and is in all ways pleasant, interesting, and, I may say, educational."

"Educational, eh?" laughed the Bibliomaniac. "Some people have queer ideas of what is educational. I must say I fail to see anything particularly instructive in flat-hunting."

"That's because you never approached it in a proper spirit," said the Idiot. "Anybody who is at all interested in sociology, however, cannot help but find instruction in a contemplation of how people are housed. You can't get any idea of how the other halves live by reading the society news in the Sunday newspapers or peeping in at the second story of the tenement-houses as you go down-town on the elevated railroads. You've got to go out and investigate for yourself, and that's where flat-hunting comes in as an educational diversion. Of course, all men are not interested in the same line of investigation. You, as a bibliomaniac, prefer to go hunting rare first editions; Dr. Pellet, armed to the teeth with capsules, lies in wait for a pot-shot at some new kind of human ailment, and rejoices as loudly over the discovery of a new disease as you do over finding a copy of the rare first edition of the *Telephone Book for 1899*; another man goes to Africa to investigate the condition of our gorillan cousin of the jungle; Lieutenant Peary goes and hides behind a snow-ball up North, so that his fellows of the Arctic Exploration Society may have something to look for every other summer; and I—I go hunting for flats. I don't sneer at you and the others for liking the things you do. You shouldn't sneer at me for liking the things I do. It is, after all, the diversity of our tastes that makes our human race interesting."

"But the rest of us generally bag something," said the Lawyer. "What the dickens do you get beyond sheer physical weariness for your pains?"

"The best of all the prizes of the hunt," said the Idiot; "the spirit of content with my lot as a boarder. I've been through twenty-eight flats in the last three weeks, and I know whereof I speak. I have seen the gorgeous apartments of the Redmere, where you can get a Louis Quinze drawing-room, a Renaissance library, a superb Grecian dining-room, and a cold-storage box to keep your high-balls in for four thousand dollars per annum."

"Weren't there any bedrooms?" asked Mr. Whitechoker.

"Oh yes," said the Idiot. "Three, automatically ventilated from holes in the ceiling leading to an air-shaft, size six by nine, and brilliantly lighted by electricity. There was also a small pigeon-hole in a corrugated iron shack on the roof for the cook; a laundry next to the coal-bin in the cellar; and a kitchen about four feet square connecting with the library."

"Mercy!" cried Mrs. Pedagog. "Do they expect children to live in such a place as that?"

"No," said the Idiot. "You have to give bonds as security against children of any kind at the Redmere. If you happen to have any, you are required by the terms of your lease to send them to boarding-school; and if you haven't any, the lease requires that you shall promise to have none during your tenancy. The owners of such properties have a lot of heart about them, and they take good care to protect the children against the apartments they put up."

"And what kind of people, pray, live in such places as that?" demanded the Bibliomaniac.

"Very nice people," said the Idiot. "People, for the most part, who spend their winters at Palm Beach, their springs in London, their summers at Newport or on the Continent, and their autumns in the Berkshires."

"I don't see why they need a home at all if that's the way they do," said Mrs. Pedagog.

"It's very simple," said the Idiot. "You've got to have an address to get your name in the *Social Register*."

"Four thousand dollars is pretty steep for an address," commented the Bibliomaniac.

"It would be for me," said the Idiot. "But it is cheap for them. Moreover, in the case of the Redmere it's the swellest address in town. Three of the most important divorces of the last social season took place at the Redmere. Social position comes high, Mr. Bib, but there are people who must have it. It is to them what baked beans are to the Bostonian's Sunday breakfast—a sine qua non."

"May I ask whatever induced you to look for a four-thousand-dollar apartment?" asked Mr. Pedagog. "You have frequently stated that your income barely equalled twenty-four hundred dollars a year."

"Why shouldn't I?" asked the Idiot. "It doesn't cost any more to look for a four-thousand-dollar apartment than it does to go chasing after a two-dollar-a-week hall-bedroom, and it impresses the cab-driver with a sense of responsibility. But bagging these gorgeous apartments does not constitute the real joy of flat-hunting. For solid satisfaction and real sport the chase for a fifteen-hundred-dollar apartment in a decent neighborhood bears away the palm. You can get plenty of roomy suites in the neighborhood of a boiler-factory, or next door to a distillery, or back of a fire-engine house, at reasonable rents, and along the elevated railway lines much that is impressive is to be found by those who can sleep with trains running alongside of their pillows all night; but when you get away from these, the real thing at that figure is elusive. Over by the Park you can get two pigeon-holes and a bath, with a southern exposure, for nineteen hundred dollars a year; if you are willing to dispense with the southern exposure you can get three Black Holes of Calcutta and a butler's pantry, in the same neighborhood, for sixteen hundred dollars, but you have to provide your own air. Farther down-town you will occasionally find the thing you want with a few extras in the shape of cornet-players, pianola-bangers, and peroxide sopranos on either side of you, and an osteopathic veterinary surgeon on the ground floor thrown in. Then there are paper flats that can be had for twelve hundred dollars, but you can't have any pictures in them, because the walls won't stand the weight, and any nail of reasonable length would stick through into the next apartment. A friend of mine lived in one of these affairs once, and when he inadvertently leaned against the wall one night he fell through into his neighbor's bath-tub. Of course, that sort of thing promotes sociability; but for a home most people want just a little privacy. And so the list runs on. You would really be astonished at the great variety of discomfortable dwelling-places that people build. Such high-art decorations as you encounter—purple friezes surmounting yellow dadoes; dragons peeping out of fruit-baskets; idealized tomatoes in full bloom chasing one another all around the bedroom walls. Then the architectural inconveniences they present with their best bedrooms opening into the kitchen; their parlors with marble wash-stands with running water in the corner; their libraries fitted up with marvellous steam-radiators and china-closets, and their kitchens so small that the fire in the range scorches the wall opposite, and over which nothing but an asbestos cook, with a figure like a third rail, could preside. And, best of all, there are the janitors! Why, Mr. Bib, the study of the janitor and his habits alone is worthy of the life-long attention of the best entomologist that ever lived—and yet you say there is nothing educational in flat-hunting."

"Oh, well," said the Bibliomaniac, "I meant for me. There are a lot of things that would be educational to you that I should regard as symptomatic of profound ignorance. Everything is relative in this world."

"That is true," said the Idiot; "and that is why every April 1st I go out and gloat over the miseries of the flat-dwellers. As long as I can do that I am happy in my little cubby-hole under Mrs. Pedagog's hospitable roof."

"Ah! I am glad to hear you say that," said Mrs. Pedagog. "I was a bit fearful, Mr. Idiot, that you had it in mind to move away from us."

"No indeed, Mrs. Pedagog," replied the Idiot, rising from the table. "You need have no fear of that. You couldn't get me out of here with a crow-bar. If I did not have entire confidence in your lovely house and yourself, you don't suppose I would permit myself to get three months behind in my board, do you?"

CHAPTER X

THE HOUSEMAID'S UNION

"POTATOES, sir?" said Mary, the waitress at Mrs. Smithers-Pedagog's High-Class Home for Single Gentlemen, stopping behind the Idiot's chair and addressing the back of his neck in the usual boarding-house fashion.

"Yes, I want some potatoes, Mary; but before I take them," the Idiot replied, "I must first ascertain whether or not you wear the union label, and what is the exact status also of the potatoes. My principles are such that I cannot permit a non-union housemaid to help me to a scab potato, whereas, if you belong to the sisterhood, and our stewed friend Murphy here has been raised upon a union farm, then, indeed, do I wish not only one potato but many."

Mary's reply was a giggle.

"Ah!" said the Idiot. "The merry ha-ha, eh? All right, Mary. That is for the present sufficient evidence that your conscience is clear on this very important matter. As for the potatoes, we will eat them not exactly under protest, but with a distinctly announced proviso in advance that we assume that they have qualified themselves for admission into a union stomach. I hesitate to think of what will happen in my interior department if Murphy is deceiving us."

Whereupon the Idiot came into possession of a goodly portion of the stewed potatoes, and Mary fled to the kitchen, where she informed the presiding genius of the range that the young gentleman was crazier than ever.

"He's talkin' about the unions, now, Bridget," said she.

"Is he agin 'em?" demanded Bridget, with a glitter in her eye.

"No, he's for 'em; he wouldn't even drink milk from a non-union cow," said Mary.

"He's a foine gintleman," said Bridget. "Oi'll make his waffles a soize larger."

Meanwhile the Bibliomaniac had chosen to reflect seriously upon the Idiot's intelligence for his approval of unions.

"They are responsible for pretty nearly all the trouble there is at the present moment," he snapped out, angrily.

"Oh, go along with you," retorted the Idiot. "The trouble we have these days, like all the rest of the troubles of the past, go right back to that old original non-union apple that Eve ate and Adam got the core of. You know that as well as I do. Even Adam and Eve, untutored children of nature though they were, saw it right off, and organized a union on the spot, which has in the course of centuries proven the most beneficent institution of the ages. With all due respect to the character of this dwelling-place of ours—a home for single gentlemen—the union is the thing. If you don't belong to one you may be tremendously independent, but you're blooming lonesome."

"The matrimonial union," smiled Mrs. Pedagog, "is indeed a blessed institution, and, having been married twice, I can testify from experience; but, truly, Mr. Idiot, I wish you wouldn't put notions into Mary's head about the other kind. I should be sorry if she were to join that housemaid's union we hear so much about. I have trouble enough now with my domestic help without having a walking delegate on my hands as well."

"No doubt," acquiesced the Idiot. "In their beginnings all great movements have their inconveniences, but in the end, properly developed, a housemaid's union wouldn't be a bad thing for employers, and I rather think it might prove a good thing. Suppose one of your servants misbehaves herself, for instance—I remember one occasion in this very house when it required the united efforts of yourself, Mr. Pedagog, three policemen, and your humble servant to effectively discharge a three-hundred-pound queen of the kitchen, who had looked not wisely but too often on the cooking sherry. Now suppose that highly cultivated inebriate had belonged to a self-respecting union? You wouldn't have had to discharge her at all. A telephone message to the union headquarters, despatched while the lady was indulging in one of her tantrums, would have brought an inspector to the house, the queen would have been caught with the goods on, and her card would have been taken from her, so that by the mere automatic operation of the rules of her own organization she could no longer work for you. Thus you would have been spared some highly seasoned language which I have for years tried to forget; Mr. Pedagog's eye would not have been punched so that you could not tell your blue-eyed boy from your black-eyed babe; I should never have lost the only really satisfactory red necktie I ever owned; and three sturdy policemen, one of whom had often previously acted as the lady's brother on her evenings at home, and the others, of whom we had reason to believe were cousins not many times removed, would not have been confronted by the ungrateful duty of clubbing one who had frequently fed them generously upon your cold mutton and my beer."

"Is that one of the things the union would do?" queried Mrs. Pedagog, brightening.

"It is one of the things the union *should* do," said the Idiot. "Similarly with your up-stairs girl, if perchance you have one. Suppose she got into the habit, which I understand is not all an uncommon case, of sweeping the dust under the bureau of your bedroom or under the piano in the drawing-room. Suppose she is really an adept in the art of dust concealment, having a full comprehension of all sixty methods—hiding it under tables, sofas, bookcases, and rugs, in order to save her back? You wouldn't have to bother with her at all under a properly equipped union. Upon the discovery of her delinquencies you would merely have to send for the union inspector, lift up the rug and show her the various vintages of sweepings the maid has left there: November ashes; December match-ends; threads, needles, and pins left over from the February meeting of the Ibsen Sewing-Circle at your house; your missing tortoise-shell hair-pin that you hadn't laid eyes on since September; the grocer's bill for October that you told the grocer you never received—all this in March. Do you suppose that that inspector, with all this evidence before her eyes, could do otherwise than prefer charges against the offender at the next meeting of the Committee on Discipline? Not on your life, madam. And, what is more, have you the slightest doubt that one word of reprimand from that same Committee on Discipline would prove far more effective in reforming that particular offender than anything you could say backed by the eloquence of Burke and the thunderbolts of Jove?"

"You paint a beautiful picture," said the Doctor. "But suppose you happened to draw a rotten cook in the domestic lottery—a good woman, but a regular scorcher. Where does your inspector come in there? Going to invite her to dine with you so as to demonstrate the girl's incompetence?"

"Not at all," said the Idiot. "That would make trouble right away. The cook very properly would say that the inspector was influenced by the social attention she was receiving from the head of the house, and the woman's effectiveness as a disciplinarian would be immediately destroyed. I'd put half portions of the burned food in a sealed package and send it to the Committee on Culinary Improvement for their inspection. A better method which time would probably bring into practice would be for the union itself to establish a system of domiciliary visits, by which the cook's work should be subjected to a constant inspection by the union—the object being, of course, to prevent trouble rather than to punish after the event. The inspector's position would be something like that of the bank examiner, who turns up at our financial institutions at unexpected moments, and sees that everything is going right."

"Oh, bosh!" said the Doctor. "You are talking of ideals."

"Certainly I am," returned the Idiot. "Why shouldn't I? What's the use of wasting one's breath on anything else?"

"Well, it's all rot!" put in Mr. Brief. "There never was any such union as that, and there never will be."

"You are the last person in the world to say a thing like that, Mr. Brief," said the Idiot—"you, who belong to the nearest approach to the ideal union that the world has ever known!"

"What! Me?" demanded the Lawyer. "Me? I belong to a union?"

"Of course you do—or at least you told me you did," said the Idiot.

"Well, you are the worst!" retorted Mr. Brief, angrily. "When did I ever tell you that I belonged to a union?"

"Last Friday night at dinner, and in the presence of this goodly company," said the Idiot. "You were bragging about it, too—said that no institution in existence had done more to uplift the moral tone of the legal profession; that through its efforts the corrupt practitioner and the shyster were gradually being driven to the wall—"

"Well, this beats me," said Mr. Brief. "I recall telling at dinner on Friday night about the Bar Association—"

"Precisely," said the Idiot. "That's what I referred to. If the Bar Association isn't a Lawyer's Union Number Six of the highest type, I don't know what is. It is conducted by the most brilliant minds in the profession; its honors are eagerly sought after by the brainiest laborers in the field of Coke and Blackstone; its stern, relentless eye is fixed upon the evil-doer, and it is an effective instrument for reform not only in its own profession, but in the State as well. What I would have the Housemaid's Union do for domestic servants and for the home, the Bar Association does for the legal profession and for the State, and if the lawyers can do this thing there is no earthly reason why the housemaids shouldn't."

"Pah!" ejaculated Mr. Brief. "You place the bar and domestic service on the same plane of importance, do you?"

"No, I don't," said the Idiot. "Shouldn't think of doing so. Twenty people need housemaids, where one requires a lawyer; therefore the domestic is the more important of the two."

"Humph!" said Mr. Brief, with an angry laugh. "Intellectual qualifications, I suppose, go for nothing in the matter."

"Well, I don't know about that," said the Idiot. "I guess, however, that there are more housemaids earning a living to-day than lawyers—and, besides—oh, well, never mind—What's the use? I don't wish to quarrel about it."

"Go on—don't mind me—I'm really interested to know what further you can say," snapped Mr. Brief. "Besides—what?"

"Only this, that when it comes to the intellectuals—Well, really, Mr. Brief," asked the Idiot, "really now, did you ever hear of anybody going to an intelligence office for a lawyer?"

Mr. Brief's reply was not inaudible, for just at that moment he swallowed his coffee the wrong way, and in the effort to bring him to, the thread of the argument snapped, and up to the hour of going to press had not been tied together again.

CHAPTER XI

THE GENTLE ART OF BOOSTING

THE Idiot was very late at breakfast—so extremely late, in fact, that some apprehension was expressed by his fellow-boarders as to the state of his health.

"I hope he isn't ill," said Mr. Whitechoker. "He is usually so prompt at his meals that I fear something is the matter with him."

"He's all right," said the Doctor, whose room adjoins that of the Idiot in Mrs. Smithers-Pedagog's Select Home for Single Gentlemen. "He'll be down in a minute. He's suffering from an overdose of vacation—rested too hard."

Just then the subject of the conversation appeared in the doorway, pale and haggard, but with an eye that boded ill for the larder.

"Quick!" he cried, as he entered. "Lead me to a square meal. Mary, please give me four bowls of mush, ten medium soft-boiled eggs, a barrel of saute potatoes, and eighteen dollars' worth of corned-beef hash. I'll have two pots of coffee, Mrs. Pedagog, please, four pounds of sugar, and a can of condensed milk. If there is any extra charge you may put it on the bill, and some day, when the common stock of the Continental Hen Trust goes up thirty or forty points, I'll pay."

"What's the matter with you, Mr. Idiot?" asked Mr. Brief. "Been fasting for a week?"

"No," replied the Idiot. "I've just taken my first week's vacation, and, between you and me, I've come back to business so as to get rested for the second."

"Doesn't look as though vacation agreed with you," said the Bibliomaniac.

"It doesn't," said the Idiot. "Hereafter I am an advocate of the rest-while-you-work system. Never take a day off if you can help it. There's nothing so restful as paying attention to business, and no greater promoter of weariness of spirit and vexation of your digestion than the modern style of vacating. No more for mine, if you please."

"Humph!" sneered the Bibliomaniac. "I suppose you went to Coney Island to get rested up, bumping the bump and looping the loop, and doing a lot of other crazy things."

"Not I," quoth the Idiot. "I didn't have sense enough to go to some quiet place like Coney Island, where you can get seven square meals a day, and then climb into a Ferris-wheel and be twirled around in the air until they have been properly shaken down. I took one of the Four Hundred vacations. Know what that is?"

"No," said Mr. Brief. "I didn't know there were four hundred vacations with only three hundred and sixty-five days in the year. What do you mean?"

"I mean the kind of vacation the people in the Four Hundred take," explained the Idiot. "I've been to a house-party up in Newport with some friends of mine who're 'in the swim,' and I tell you it's hard swimming. You'll never hear me talking about a leisure class in this country again. Those people don't know what leisure is. I don't wonder they're always such a tired-looking lot."

"I was not aware that you were in with the Smart Set," said the Bibliomaniac.

"Oh yes," said the Idiot. "I'm in with several of 'em—'way in; so far in that I'm sometimes afraid I'll never get out. We're carrying a whole lot of wild-cats on margin for Billie Van Gelder, the cotillon leader. Tommy de Cahoots, the famous yachtsman, owes us about eight thousand dollars more than he can spare from his living expenses on one of his plunges into Copper, and altogether we are pretty long on swells in our office."

"And do you mean to say those people invite you out?" asked the Bibliomaniac.

"All the time," said the Idiot. "Just as soon as one of our swell customers finds he can't pay his margins he comes down to the office and gets very chummy with all of us. The deeper he is in it the more affable he becomes. The result is there are house-parties and yacht-cruises and all that sort of thing galore on tap for us every summer."

"And you accept them, eh?" said the Bibliomaniac, scornfully.

"As a matter of business, of course," replied the Idiot. "We've got to get something out of it. If one of our customers can't pay cash, why, we get what we can. In this particular case Mr. Reginald Squandercash had me down at Newport for five full days, and I know now why he can't pay up his little shortage of eight hundred dollars. He's got the money, but he needs it for other things, and, now that I know it, I shall recommend the firm to give him an extension of thirty days. By that time he will have collected from the De Boodles, whom he is launching in society, C. O. D., and will be able to square matters with us."

"Your conversation is Greek to me," said the Bibliomaniac. "Who are the De Boodles, and for what do they owe your friend Reginald Squandercash money?"

"The De Boodles," explained the Idiot, "are what are known as climbers, and Reginald Squandercash is a booster."

"A what?" cried the Bibliomaniac.

"A booster," said the Idiot. "There are several boosters in the Four Hundred. For a consideration they will boost wealthy climbers into society. The climbers are people like the De Boodles, who have suddenly come into great wealth, and who wish to be in it with others of great wealth who are also of high social position. They don't know how to do the trick, so they seek out some booster like Reggie, strike a bargain with him, and he steers 'em up against the 'Among-Those-Present' game until finally you find the De Boodles have a social cinch."

"Do you mean to say that society tolerates such a business as that?" demanded the Bibliomaniac.

"Tolerates?" laughed the Idiot. "What a word to use! Tolerate? Why, society encourages, because society shares the benefits. Take this especial vacation of mine. Society had two five-o'clock teas, four of the swellest dinners you ever sat down to, a cotillon where the favors were of solid silver and real ostrich feathers, a whole day's clam-bake on Reggie's steam-yacht, with automobile-runs and coaching-trips galore. Nobody ever declines one of Reggie's invitations, because what he has from a society point of view is the best the market affords. Why, the floral decorations alone at the fête champêtre he gave in honor of the De Boodles at his villa last Thursday night must have cost five thousand dollars, and everything was on the same scale. I don't believe a cent less than seventy-five hundred dollars was burned up in the fire-works, and every lady present received a souvenir of the occasion that cost at least one hundred dollars."

"Your story doesn't quite hold together," said Mr. Brief. "If your friend Reggie has a villa and a steam-yacht, and automobiles and coaches, and gives fêtes champêtres that cost fifteen or twenty thousand dollars, I don't see why he has to make himself a booster of inferior people who want to get into society. What does he gain by it? It surely isn't sport to do a thing like that, and I should think he'd find it a dreadful bore."

"The man must live," said the Idiot. "He boosts for a living."

"When he has the wealth of Monte Cristo at his command?" demanded Mr. Brief.

"Reggie hasn't a cent to his name," said the Idiot. "I've already told you he owes us eight hundred dollars he can't pay."

"Then who in thunder pays for the villa and the lot and all those hundred-dollar souvenirs?" asked the Doctor.

"Why, this year, the De Boodles," said the Idiot. "Last year it was Colonel and Mrs. Moneybags, whose daughter, Miss Fayette Moneybags, is now clinching the position Reggie sold her at Newport over in London, whither Reggie has consigned her to his sister, an impecunious American duchess—the Duchess of Nocash—who is also in the boosting business. The chances are Miss Moneybags will land one of England's most deeply indebted peers, and, if she does, Reggie will receive a handsome check for steering the family up against so attractive a proposition."

"And you mean to tell us that a plain man like old John De Boodle, of Nevada, is putting out his hard-earned wealth in that way?" demanded Mr. Brief.

"I didn't mean to mention any names," said the Idiot. "But you've spotted the victim. Old John De Boodle, who made his sixty million dollars in six months, after having kept a saloon on the frontier for forty years, is the man. His family wants to get in the swim, and Reggie is turning the trick for them; and, after all, what better way is there for De Boodle to get in? He might take sixty villas at Newport and not get even a peep at the divorce colony there, much less a glimpse of the monogamous set acting independently. Not a monkey in the Zoo would dine with the De Boodles, and in his most eccentric moment I doubt if Tommy Dare would take them up, unless there was somebody to stand sponsor for them. A cool million might easily be expended without results by the De Boodles themselves; but hand that money over to Reggie Squandercash, whose blood is as blue as his creditors' sometimes get, and you can look for results. What the Frohman's are to the stage, Reggie Squandercash is to society. He's right in it; popular as all spenders are; lavish as all people spending other people's money are apt to be. Old De Boodle, egged on by Mrs. De Boodle and Miss Mary Ann De Boodle (now known as Miss Marianne De Boodle), goes to Reggie and says: 'The old lady and my girl are nutty on society. Can you land 'em?' 'Certainly,' says Reggie, 'if your pocket is long enough.' 'How long is that?' asks De Boodle, wincing a bit. 'A hundred thousand a month, and no extras, until you're in,' says Reggie. 'No reduction for families?' asks De Boodle, anxiously. 'No,' says Reggie. 'Harder job.' 'All right,' says De Boodle, 'here's my check for the first month.' That's how Reggie gets his Newport villa, his servants, his horses, yacht, automobiles, and coaches. Then he invites the De Boodles up to visit him. They accept, and the fun begins. First it's a little dinner to meet my friends Mr. and Mrs. De Boodle, of Nevada. Everybody there, hungry, dinner from Sherry's, best wines in the market. De Boodles covered with diamonds, a great success, especially old John De Boodle, who tells racy stories over the demi-tasse when the ladies have gone into the drawing-room. De Boodle voted a character. Next thing, bridge-whist party. Everybody there. Society a good winner. The De Boodles magnificent losers. Popularity cinched. Next, yachting-party. Everybody on board. De Boodle on deck in fine shape. Champagne flows like Niagara. Poker game in main cabin. Food everywhere. De Boodles much easier. Stiffness wearing off, and so on and so on, until finally Miss De Boodle's portrait is printed in nineteen Sunday newspapers all over the country. They're launched, and Reggie comes into his own with a profit for the season in a cash balance of fifty thousand dollars. He's had a bully time all summer, entertained like a prince, and comes to the rainy season with a tidy little umbrella to keep him out of the wet."

"And can he count on that as a permanent business?" asked Mr. Whitechoker.

"My dear sir, the rock of Gibraltar is no solider and no more permanent," said the Idiot. "For as long as there is a Four Hundred in existence, human nature is such that there will also be a million who will want to get into it."

"At such a cost?" demanded the Bibliomaniac.

"At any cost," replied the Idiot. "Even people who know they cannot swim want to get in it."

CHAPTER XII

HE MAKES A SUGGESTION TO THE POET

"GOOD-MORNING, Homer, my boy," said the Idiot, genially, as the Poet entered the breakfast-room. "All hail to thee. Thou art the bright particular bird of plumage I most hoped to see this rare and beauteous summer morning. No sweet-singing robin-redbreast or soft-honking canvasback for yours truly this A.M., when a living, breathing, palpitating son of the Muses lurks near at hand. I fain would make thee a proposition, Shakespeare dear!"

"Back pedal there! Avaunt with your flowery speech, oh Idiot!" cried the Doctor. "Else will I call an ambulance."

"No ambulance for mine," chortled the Idiot.

"Nay, Sweet Gas-bags," quoth the Doctor. "But for once I fear me we may be scorched by this Pelée of words that thou spoutest forth."

"What's the proposition, Mr. Idiot?" asked the Poet. "I'm always open to anything of the kind, as the Subway said when an automobile fell into it.'"

"I thirst for laurels," said the Idiot, "and I propose that you and I collaborate on a book of poems for early publication. With your name on the title-page and my poems in the book I think we can make a go of it."

"What's the lay?" asked the Poet, amused, but wary. "Sonnets, or French forms, or just plain snatches of song?"

"Any old thing as long as it runs smoothly," replied the Idiot. "Only the poems must fit the title of the book, which is to be *Now*."

"*Now?*" said the Poet.

"*Now!*" repeated the Idiot. "I find in reading over the verse of the day that the 'Now' poem always finds a ready market. Therefore, there must be money in it, and where the money goes there the laurels are. You know what Browning Robinson, the Laureate of Wall Street, wrote in his 'Message to Posterity':

> " '*Oh,   my brow,*
> *Bring me no bay nor sorrel;*
> *Give me no parsley wreath, but just*
> *The legal long green laurel.* '"

"I never heard that poem before," laughed the Poet, "though the sentiment in these commercial days is not unfamiliar."

"True," said the Idiot. "Alfred Austin Biggs, of Texas, voiced the same idea when he said:

> "'Crown me not with spinach,
> Wreathe me not with hay;
> Place no salad on my head
> When you bring the bay.
> Give me not the water-cresses
> To adorn my flowing tresses,
> But at e'en
> Crown my pockets good and strong
> With the green—
> The green that's long.'"

"Do you remember that?" asked the Idiot.

"Only faintly," said the Poet. "I think you read it to me once before, just after you—er—ah—rather just after Alfred Austin Biggs, of Texas—wrote it."

The Idiot laughed. "I see you're on," he said. "Anyhow, it's good sentiment, whether I wrote it or Biggs. Fact is, in my judgment, what the poet of to-day ought to do is to collect the long green from the present and the laurel from posterity. That's a fair division. But what do you say to my proposition?"

"Well, it's certainly—er—cheeky enough," said the Poet. "Do I understand it?—you want me to father your poems. To tell the truth, until I hear some of them, I can't promise to be more than an uncle to them."

"That's all right," said the Idiot. "You ought to be cautious, as a matter of protection to your own name. I've got some of the goods right here. Here's a little thing called 'Summer-tide!' It shows the whole 'Now' principle in a nutshell. Listen to this:

> "Now the festive frog is croaking in the mere,
>   And the canvasback is honking in the bay,
> And the summer-girl is smiling full of cheer
>   On the willieboys that chance along her way.

> "Now the skeeter sings his carols to the dawn,
>   And bewails the early closing of the bar
> That prevents the little nips he seeks each morn
>   On the sea-shore where the fatling boarders are.

"Now the landlord of the pastoral hotel
Spends his mornings, nights, and eke his afternoons,
Scheming plans to get more milk from out the well,
And a hundred novel ways of cooking prunes.

"Now the pumpkin goes a pumpking through the fields,
And the merry visaged cows are chewing cud;
And the profits that the plumber's business yields
Come a-tumbling to the earth with deadly thud.

"And from all of this we learn the lesson sweet,
The soft message of Dame Nature, grand and clear,
That the winter-time is gone with storm and sleet,
And the soft and jolly summer-tide is here.

How's that? Pretty fair?"

"Well, I might consent to be a cousin to a poem of that kind. I've read worse and written some that are quite as bad. But you know, Mr. Idiot, even so great a masterpiece as that won't make a book," said the Poet.

"Of course it won't," retorted the Idiot. "That's only for the summer. Here's another one on winter. Just listen:

"Now the man who deals in mittens and in tabs
Is a-smiling broadly—aye, from ear to ear—
As he reaches out his hand and fondly grabs
All the shining, golden shekels falling near.

"Now the snow lies on the hill-side and the roof,
And the birdling to the sunny southland flies;
While the frowning summer landlord stands aloof,
And to solemncholy meditation hies.

"Now the tinkling of the sleigh-bells tinge the air,
And the coal-man is as happy as can be;
While the hulking, sulking, grizzly seeks his lair,
And the ice-man's soul is filled with misery.

"Clad in frost are all the distant mountain-peaks,
And the furnace is as hungry as a boy;
While the plumber, as he gloats upon the leaks,
Is the model that the painter takes for 'Joy.'

> *"And from all of this we learn the lesson sweet—*
> *The glad message of Dame Nature, grand and clear:*
> *That the summer-time has gone with all its heat,*
> *And the crisp and frosty winter days are here.*

You see, Mr. Poet, that out of that one idea alone—that cataloguing of the things of the four seasons—you can get four poems that are really worth reading," said the Idiot. "We could call that section 'The Seasons,' and make it the first part of the book. In the second part we could do the same thing, only in greater detail, for each one of the months. Just as a sample, take the month of February. We could run something like this in on February:

> *"Now o'er the pavement comes a hush*
> *As pattering feet wade deep in slush*
> *That every Feb.*
> *Doth flow and ebb."*

"I see," said the Poet. "It wouldn't take long to fill up a book with stuff like that."

"To make the appeal stronger, let me take the month of July, which is now on," resumed the Idiot. "You may find it even more convincing:

> *"Now the fly—*
> *The rhubarb-pie—*
> *The lightning in the sky—*
> *Thermometers so spry—*
> *That leap up high—*
> *The roads all dry,*
> *The hoboes nigh,*
> *The town a-fry,*
> *The mad ki-yi*
> *A-snarling by,*
> *The crickets cry—*
> *All tell us that it is July.*

Eh?"

"I don't believe anybody would believe I wrote it, that's all," said the Poet, shaking his head dubiously. "They'd find out, sooner or later, that you did it, just as they discovered that Will Carleton wrote 'Paradise Lost,' and Dick Davis was the real author of Shakespeare. Why don't you publish the thing over your own name?"

"Too modest," said the Idiot. "What do you think of this:

> *"Now the festive candidate*
> *Goes a-sporting through the State,*
> *And he kisses babes from Quogue to Kalamazoo;*
> *For he really wants to win*
> *Without spending any tin,*
> *And he thinks he has a chance to kiss it through."*

"That's fair, only I don't think you'll find many candidates doing that sort of thing nowadays," said the Poet. "Most public men I know of would rather spend their money than kiss the babies. That style of campaigning has gone out."

"It has in the cities," said the Idiot. "But back in the country it is still done, and the candidate who turns his back on the infant might as well give up the race. I know, because a cousin of mine ran for supervisor once, and he was licked out of his boots because he tried to do his kissing by proxy—said he'd give the kisses in a bunch to a committee of young ladies, who could distribute them for him. Result was everybody was down on him—even the young ladies."

"I guess he was a cousin of yours, all right," laughed the Doctor; "that scheme bears the Idiot brand."

"Here's one on the opening of the opera season," said the Idiot:

> *"Now the fiddlers tune their fiddles*
> *To the lovely taradiddles*
> *Of old Wagner, Mozart, Bizet, and the rest.*
> *Now the trombone is a-tooting*
> *Out its scaley shute-the-chuteing*
> *And the oboe is hoboing with a zest.*

> *"Now the dressmakers are working—*
> *Not a single minute shirking—*
> *Making gowns with frills and fal-lals mighty queer,*
> *For the Autumn days are flying,*
> *And there's really no denying*
> *That the season of the opera is near."*

Mr. Brief took a hand in the discussion at this moment.

"Then you can have a blanket verse," he said, scribbling with his pencil on a piece of paper in front of him. "Something like this:

> *"And as Time goes on a-stalking,*
> *And the Idiot still is talking*
> *In his usual blatant manner, loud and free,*
> *With his silly jokes and rhyme,*
> *It is—well it's any time*
> *From Creation to the jumping-off place that you'll find at the far*
> *end of Eterni-tie."*

"That settles it," said the Idiot, rising. "I withdraw my proposition. Let's call it off, Mr. Poet."

"What's the matter?" asked Mr. Brief. "Isn't my verse good?"

"Yes," said the Idiot. "Just as good as mine, and that being the case it isn't worth doing. When lawyers can write as good poetry as real poets, it doesn't pay to be a real poet. I'm going in for something else. I guess I'll apply for a job as a motorman, and make a name for myself there."

"Can a motorman make a name for himself?" asked the Doctor.

"Oh yes," said the Idiot. "Easily. By being civil. A civil motorman would be unique."

"But he wouldn't make a fortune," suggested the Poet.

"Yes he would, too," said the Idiot. "If he could prove he really was civil, the vaudeville people would pay him a thousand dollars a week and tour the country with him. He'd draw mobs."

With which the Idiot left the dining-room.

"I think his poems would sell," smiled Mrs. Pedagog.

"Yes," said Mr. Pedagog. "Chopped up fine and properly advertised, they might make a very successful new kind of breakfast food—provided the paper on which they were written was not too indigestible."

CHAPTER XIII

HE DISCUSSES THE MUSIC CURE

"GOOD-MORNING, Doctor," said the Idiot, as Capsule, M.D., entered the dining-room, "I am mighty glad you've come. I've wanted for a long time to ask you about this music cure that everybody is talking about, and get you, if possible, to write me out a list of musical nostrums for every-day use. I noticed last night, before going to bed, that my medicine-chest was about run out. There's nothing but one quinine pill and a soda-mint drop left in it, and if there's anything in the music cure, I don't think I'll have it filled again. I prefer Wagner to squills, and, compared to the delights of Mozart, Hayden, and Offenbach, those of paregoric are nit."

"Still rambling, eh?" vouchsafed the Doctor. "You ought to submit your tongue to some scientific student of dynamics. I am inclined to think, from my own observation of its ways, that it contains the germ of perpetual motion."

"I will consider your suggestion," replied the Idiot. "Meanwhile, let us consult harmoniously together on the original point. Is there anything in this music cure, and is it true that our medical schools are hereafter to have conservatories attached to them, in which aspiring young M.D.'s are to be taught the materia musica in addition to the materia medica?"

"I had heard of no such idiotic proposition," returned the Doctor. "And as for the music cure, I don't know anything about it; haven't heard everybody talking about it; and doubt the existence of any such thing outside of that mysterious realm which is bounded by the four corners of your own bright particular cerebellum. What do you mean by the music cure?"

"Why, the papers have been full of it lately," explained the Idiot. "The claim is made that in music lies the panacea for all human ills. It may not be able to perform a surgical operation like that which is required for the removal of a leg, and I don't believe even Wagner ever composed a measure that could be counted on successfully to eliminate one's vermiform appendix from its chief sphere of usefulness; but for other things, like measles, mumps, the snuffles, or indigestion, it is said to be wonderfully efficacious. What I wanted to find out from you was just what composers were best for which specific troubles."

"You'll have to go to somebody else for the information," said the Doctor. "I never heard of the theory, and, as I said before, I don't believe anybody else has, barring your own sweet self."

"I have seen a reference to it somewhere," put in Mr. Whitechoker, coming to the Idiot's rescue. "As I recall the matter, some lady had been cured of a nervous affection by a scientific application of some musical poultice or other, and the general expectation seems to be that some day we shall find in music a cure for all our human ills, as the Idiot suggests."

"Thank you, Mr. Whitechoker," said the Idiot, gratefully ratefuly. "I saw that same item and several others besides, and I have only told the truth when I say that a large number of people are considering the possibilities of music as a substitute for drugs. I am surprised that Dr. Capsule has neither heard nor thought about it, for I should think it would prove to be a pleasant and profitable field for speculation. Even I, who am only a dabbler in medicine and know no more about it than the effects of certain remedies upon my own symptoms, have noticed that music of a certain sort is a sure emollient for nervous conditions."

"For example?" said the Doctor. "Of course, we don't doubt your word; but when a man makes a statement based upon personal observation it is profitable to ask him what his precise experience has been, merely for the purpose of adding to our own knowledge."

"Well," said the Idiot, "the first instance that I can recall is that of a Wagner opera and its effects upon me. For a number of years I suffered a great deal from insomnia. I could not get two hours of consecutive sleep, and the effect of my sufferings was to make me nervous and irritable. Suddenly somebody presented me with a couple of tickets for a performance of 'Parsifal,' and I went. It began at five o'clock in the afternoon. For twenty minutes all went serenely, and then the music began to work. I fell into a deep and refreshing slumber. The intermission came, and still I slept on. Everybody else went home, dressed for the evening part of the performance, had their dinner, and returned. Still I slept, and continued so to do until midnight, when one of the gentlemanly ushers came and waked me up, and told me that the performance was over. I rubbed my eyes, and looked about me. It was true—the great auditorium was empty, and was gradually darkening. I put on my hat and walked out refreshed, having slept from five-twenty until twelve, or six hours and forty minutes straight. That was one instance. Two weeks later I went again, this time to hear 'Götterdämmerung.' The results were the same, only the effect was instantaneous. The curtain had hardly risen before I retired to the little ante-room of the box our party occupied and dozed off into a fathomless sleep. I didn't wake up this time until nine o'clock the next day, the rest of the party having gone off without awakening me as a sort of joke. Clearly Wagner, according to my way of thinking, then, deserves to rank among the most effective narcotics known to modern science. I have tried all sorts of other things—sulfonal, trionel, bromide powders, and all the rest, and not one of them produced anything like the soporific results that two doses of Wagner brought about in one instant. And, best of all, there was no reaction: no splitting headache or shaky hand the next day, but just the calm, quiet, contented feeling that goes with the sense of having got completely rested up."

"You run a dreadful risk, however," said the Doctor, with a sarcastic smile. "The Wagner habit is a terrible thing to acquire, Mr. Idiot."

"That may be," said the Idiot; "worse than the sulfonal habit by a great deal, I am told; but I am in no danger of becoming a victim to it while it costs from five to seven dollars a dose. In addition to this experience, I have also the testimony of a friend of mine who was cured of a frightful attack of the colic by Sullivan's 'Lost Chord,' played on a cornet. He had spent the day down at Asbury Park, and had eaten not wisely but too copiously. Among other things that he turned loose in his inner man were two plates of lobster salad, a glass of fresh cider, and a saucerful of pistache ice-cream. He was a painter by profession, and the color scheme he thus introduced into his digestive apparatus was too much for his artistic soul. He was not fitted by temperament to assimilate anything quite so strenuously chromatic as that, and, as a consequence, shortly after he had retired to his studio for the night, the conflicting tints began to get in their deadly work, and within two hours he was completely doubled up. The pain he suffered was awful. Agony was bliss alongside of the pangs that now afflicted him, and all the palliatives and pain-killers known to man were tried without avail, and then, just as he was about to give himself up for lost, an amateur cornetist who occupied a studio on the floor above began to play the 'Lost Chord.' A counter-pain set in immediately. At the second bar of the 'Lost Chord' the awful pain that was gradually gnawing away at his vitals seemed to lose its poignancy in the face of the greater suffering, and physical relief was instant. As the musician proceeded, the internal disorder yielded gradually to the external and finally passed away, entirely leaving him so far from prostrate that by 1 A. M. he was out of bed and actually girding himself with a shot-gun and an Indian club to go up-stairs for a physical encounter with the cornetist."

"And you reason from this that Sullivan's 'Lost Chord' is a cure for cholera morbus, eh?" sneered the Doctor.

"It would seem so," said the Idiot. "While the music continued my friend was a well man, ready to go out and fight like a warrior; but when the cornetist stopped the colic returned, and he had to fight it out in the old way. In these incidents in my own experience I find ample justification for my belief, and that of others, that some day the music cure for human ailments will be recognized and developed to the full. Families going off to the country for the summer, instead of taking a medicine-chest along with them, will be provided with a music-box with cylinders for mumps, measles, summer complaint, whooping-cough, chicken-pox, chills and fever, and all the other ills the flesh is heir to. Scientific experiment will demonstrate before long just what composition will cure specific ills. If a baby has whooping-cough, an anxious mother, instead of ringing up the doctor, will go to the piano and give the child a dose of 'Hiawatha.' If a small boy goes swimming and catches a cold in his head and is down with a fever, his nurse, an expert on the accordion, can bring him back to health again with three bars of 'Under the Bamboo Tree' after each meal. Instead of dosing the kids with cod-liver oil when they need a tonic, they will be set to work at a mechanical piano and braced up on 'Narcissus.' 'There'll Be a Hot Time in the Old Town To-night' will become an effective remedy for a sudden chill. People suffering from sleeplessness can dose themselves back to normal conditions with Wagner the way I did. Tchaikowsky, to be well shaken before taken, will be an effective remedy for a torpid liver, and the man or woman who suffers from lassitude will doubtless find in the lively airs of our two-step composers an efficient tonic to bring their vitality up to a high standard of activity. Nothing in it? Why, Doctor, there's more in it that's in sight to-day that is promising and suggestive of great things in the future than there was of the principle of gravitation in the rude act of that historic pippin that left the parent tree and swatted Sir Isaac Newton on the nose."

"And the drug stores will be driven out of business, I presume," said the Doctor.

"No," said the Idiot. "They will substitute music for drugs, that is all. Every man who can afford it will have his own medical phonograph, or music-box, and the drug stores will sell cylinders and records for them instead of quinine, carbonate of soda, squills, paregoric, and other nasty-tasting things they have now. This alone will serve to popularize sickness, and, instead of being driven out of business, their trade will pick up."

"And the doctor, and the doctor's gig, and all the appurtenances of his profession—what becomes of them?" demanded the Doctor.

"We'll have to have the doctor just the same to prescribe for us, only he will have to be a musician, but the gig—I'm afraid that will have to go," said the Idiot.

"And why, pray?" asked the Doctor. "Because there are no more drugs, must the physician walk?"

"Not at all," said the Idiot. "But he'd be better equipped if he drove about in a piano-organ or, if he preferred, an auto on a steam-calliope."

CHAPTER XIV

HE DEFENDS CAMPAIGN METHODS

"GOOD-MORNING, gentlemen," said the Idiot, cheerily, as he entered the breakfast-room. "This is a fine Sunday morning in spite of the gloom into which the approaching death of the campaign should plunge us all."

"You think that, do you?" observed the Bibliomaniac. "Well, I don't agree with you. I for one am sick and tired of politics, and it will be a great relief to me when it is all over."

"Dear me, what a blasé old customer you are, Mr. Bib," returned the Idiot. "Do you mean to say that a Presidential campaign does not keep your nerve-centres in a constant state of pleasurable titillation? Why, to me it is what a bag full of nuts must be to a squirrel. I fairly gloat over these quadrennial political campaigns of ours. They are to me among the most exhilarating institutions of modern life. They satisfy all one's zest for warfare without the distressing shedding of blood which attends real war, and regarded from the standpoint of humor, I know of nothing that, to the eye of an ordinarily keen observer, is more provocative of good, honest, wholesome mirth."

"I don't see it," said Mr. Bib. "To my mind, the average political campaign is just a vulgar scrap in which men who ought to know better descend to all sorts of despicable trickery merely to gain the emoluments of office. This quest for the flesh-pots of politics, so far from being diverting, is, to my notion, one of the most deplorable exhibitions of human weakness that modern civilization, so called, has produced. A couple of men are put up for the most dignified office known to the world—both are gentlemen by birth and education, men of honor, men who, you would think, would scorn baseness as they hate poison—and then what happens? For three weary months the followers of each attack the character and intelligence of the other until, if you really believed what was said of either, neither in your estimation would have a shred of reputation left. Is that either diverting or elevating or educational or, indeed, anything but deplorable?"

"It's perfectly fine," said the Idiot, "to think that we have men in the country whose characters are such that they can stand four months of such a test. That's what I find elevating in it. When a man who is nominated for the Presidency in June or July can emerge in November unscathed in spite of the minute scrutiny to which himself and his record and the record of his sisters and his cousins and his aunts have been subjected, it's time for the American rooster to get upon his hind legs and give three cheers for himself and the people to whom he belongs. Even old Diogenes, who spent his life looking for an honest man, would have to admit every four years that he could spot him instantly by merely coming to this country and taking his choice from among the several candidates."

"You must admit, however," said the Bibliomaniac, "that a man with an honorable name must find it unpleasant to have such outrageous stories told of him."

"Not a bit of it," laughed the Idiot. "The more outrageous the better. For instance, when *The Sunday Jigger* comes out with a four-page revelation of your Republican candidate's past, in which we learn how, in 1873, he put out the eyes of a maiden aunt with a red-hot poker, and stabbed a negro cook in the back with a skewer, because she would not permit him to put rat-poison in his grandfather's coffee, you know perfectly well that that story has been put forth for the purpose of turning the maiden aunt, negro, and grandfather votes against him. You know well enough that he either never did what is charged against him, or at least that the story is greatly exaggerated—he may have stuck a pin into the cook, and played some boyish trick upon some of his relatives—but the story on the face of it is untrue and therefore harmless. Similarly with the Democratic candidate. When the *Daily Flim Flam* asserts that he believes that the working-man is entitled to four cents a day for sixteen hours' work, and has repeatedly avowed that bread and water is the proper food for motormen, everybody with common-sense realizes at once that even the *Flim Flam* doesn't believe the story. It hurts no one, therefore, and provokes a great deal of innocent mirth. You don't yourself believe that last yarn about the Prohibition candidate, do you?"

"I haven't heard any yarn about him," said the Bibliomaniac.

"That he is the owner of a brewery up in Rochester, and backs fifteen saloons and a pool-room in New York?" said the Idiot.

"Of course I don't," said the Bibliomaniac. "Who does?"

"Nobody," said the Idiot; "and therefore the story doesn't hurt the man's reputation a bit, or interfere with his chances of election in the least. Take that other story published in a New York newspaper that on the 10th of last August Thompson Bondifeller's yacht was seen anchored for six hours off Tom Watson's farm, two hundred miles from the sea, and that the Populist candidate, disguised as a bank president, went off with the trust magnate on a cruise from Atlanta, Georgia, to Oklahoma—you don't believe that, do you?"

"It's preposterous on the face of it," said Mr. Bib.

"Well, that's the way the thing works," said the Idiot. "And that's why I think there's a lot of bully good fun to be had out of a political campaign. I love anything that arouses the imagination of a people too much given over to the pursuit of the cold, hard dollar. If it wasn't for these quadrennial political campaigns to spur the fancy on to glorious flights we should become a dull, hard, prosaic, unimaginative people, and that would be death to progress. No people can progress that lacks imagination. Politics is an emery-wheel that keeps our wits polished."

"Well, granting all that you say is true," said the Bibliomaniac, "the intrusion upon a man's private life that politics makes possible—surely you cannot condone that."

The Idiot laughed.

"That's the strangest argument of all," he said. "The very idea of a man who deliberately chooses public life as the sphere of his activities seeking to hide behind his private life is preposterous. The fellow who does that, Mr. Bib, wants to lead a double life, and that is reprehensible. The man who offers himself to the people hasn't any business to tie a string to any part of him. If Jim Jones wants to be President of the United States the people who are asked to put him there have a right to know what kind of a person Jim Jones is in his dressing-gown and slippers. If he beats his mother-in-law, and eats asparagus with the sugar-tongs, and doesn't pay his grocer, the public have a right to know it. If he has children, the voters are perfectly justified in asking what kind of children they are, since the voters own the White House furniture, and if the Jim Jones children wipe their feet on plush chairs, and shoot holes in the paintings with their bean-snappers and putty-blowers, Uncle Sam, as a landlord and owner of the premises, ought to be warned beforehand. You wouldn't yourself rent a furnished residence to a man whose children were known to have built bonfires in the parlor of their last known home, would you?"

"I think not," smiled the Bibliomaniac.

"Then you cannot complain if Uncle Sam is equally solicitous about the personal paraphernalia of the man who asks to occupy his little cottage on the Potomac," said the Idiot. "So it happens that when a man runs for the Presidency the persons who intrude upon his private life, as you put it, are conferring a real service upon their fellow-citizens. When I hear from an authentic source that Mr. So-and-So, the candidate of the Thisorthatic party for the Presidency, is married to an estimable lady who refers to all Frenchmen as parricides, because she believes they have come from Paris, I have a right to consider whether or not I wish to vote to place such a lady at the head of my official table at White House banquets, where she is likely, sooner or later, to encounter the French ambassador, and the man who gives me the necessary information is doing me a service. You may say that the lady is not running for a public office, and that, therefore, she should be protected from public scrutiny, but that is a fallacy. A man's wife is his better half and his children are a good part of the remainder, and what they do or don't do becomes a matter of legitimate public concern. As a matter of fact, a public man *can* have no private life."

"Then you approve of these stories of candidates' cousins, the prattling anecdotes of their grandchildren, these paragraphs narrating the doings of their uncles-in-law, and all that?" sneered the Bibliomaniac.

"Certainly, I do," said the Idiot. "When I hear that Judge Torkin's grandson, aged four, has come out for his grandfather's opponent I am delighted, and give the judge credit for the independent spirit which heredity accounts for; when it is told to me that Tom Watson's uncle is going to vote for Tom because he knows Tom doesn't believe what he says, I am almost inclined to vote for him as the uncle of his country; when I hear that Debs's son, aged three, has punched his daddy in the eye, on general principles I feel that there's a baby I want in the White House; and when it is told to me that the Prohibition candidate's third cousin has just been cured of delirium tremens, I feel that possibly there is a family average there that may be struck to the advantage of the country."

"Say, Mr. Idiot," put in the Poet, at this point, "who are you going to vote for, anyhow?"

"Don't ask me," laughed the Idiot. "I don't know yet. I admire all the candidates personally very much."

"But what are your politics—Republican or Democratic?" asked the Lawyer.

"Oh, that's different," said the Idiot. "I'm a Sammycrat."

"A what?" cried the Idiot's fellow-boarders in unison.

"A Sammycrat," said the Idiot. "I'm for Uncle Sam every time. He's the best ever."

CHAPTER XV

ON SHORT COURSES AT COLLEGE

MR. PEDAGOG threw down the morning paper with an ejaculation of impatience.

"I don't know what on earth we are coming to!" he said, stirring his coffee vigorously. "These new-fangled notions of our college presidents seem to me to be destructive in their tendency."

"What's up now? Somebody flunked a football team?" asked the Idiot.

"No, I quite approve of that," said Mr. Pedagog; "but this matter of reducing the college course from four to two years is so radical a suggestion that I tremble for the future of education."

"Oh, I wouldn't if I were you, Mr. Pedagog," said the Idiot. "Your trembling won't help matters any, and, after all, when men like President Eliot of Harvard and Dr. Butler of Columbia recommend the short course the idea must have some virtue."

"Well, if it stops where they do I don't suppose any great harm will be done," said Mr. Pedagog. "But what guarantee have we that fifty years from now some successor to these gentlemen won't propose a one-year course?"

"None," said the Idiot. "Fact is, we don't want any guarantee—or at least I don't. They can turn colleges into bicycle academies fifty years from now for all I care. I expect to be doing time in some other sphere fifty years from now, so why should I vex my soul about it?"

"That's rather a selfish view, isn't it, Mr. Idiot?" asked Mr. White-choker. "Don't you wish to see the world getting better and better every day?"

"No," said the Idiot. "It's so mighty good as it is, this bully old globe, that I hate to see people monkeying with it all the time. Of course, I wasn't around it in the old days, but I don't believe the world's any better off now than it was in the days of Adam."

"Great Heavens! What a thing to say!" cried the Poet.

"Well, I've said it," rejoined the Idiot. "What has it all come to, any-how—all this business of man's trying to better the world? It's just added to his expenses, that's all. And what does he get out of it that Adam didn't get? Money? Adam didn't need money. He had his garden truck, his tailor, his fuel supply, his amusements—all the things we have to pay cash for—right in his backyard. All he had to do was to reach out and take what we fellows nowadays have to toil eight or ten hours a day to earn. Literature? His position was positively enviable as far as literature is concerned. He had the situation in his own hands. He wasn't prevented from writing 'Hamlet,' as I am, because somebody else had already done it. He didn't have to sit up till midnight seven nights a week to keep up with the historical novels of the day. Art? There were pictures on every side of him, splendid in color, instinct of life, perfect in their technique, and all from the hand of that first of Old Masters, Nature herself. He hadn't any Rosa Bonheurs or Landseers on his farm, but he could get all the cow pictures he wanted from the back window of his bungalow without their costing him a cent. Drama? Life was a succession of rising curtains to Adam, and while, of course, he had the errant Eve to deal with, the garden was free from Notorious Mrs. Ebbsmiths, there wasn't a Magda from one end of the apple-orchard to the other, and not a First, Second, or Third Mrs. Tanqueray in sight. Music? The woods were full of it—the orioles singing their cantatas, the nightingales warbling their concertos, the eagles screeching out their Wagnerian measures, the blue-jays piping their intermezzos, and no Italian organ-grinders doing De Koven under his window from one year's end to the other. Gorry! I wish sometimes Adam had known a good thing when he had it and hadn't broken the monologue."

"The what?" demanded Mr. Brief.

"The monologue," repeated the Idiot. "The one commandment. If ten commandments make a decalogue, one commandment makes a mono-logue, doesn't it?"

"You're a philologist and a half," said the Bibliomaniac, with a laugh.

"No credit to me," returned the Idiot. "A ten years' residence in this boarding-house has resulted practically in my having enjoyed a diet of words. I have literally eaten syllables—"

"I hope you haven't eaten any of your own," said the Bibliomaniac. "That would ruin the digestion of an ostrich."

"That's true enough," said the Idiot. "Rich foods will overthrow any kind of a digestion in the long run. But to come back to the college ten-dencies, Mr. Pedagog, it is my belief that in this short-course business we haven't more than started. It's my firm conviction that some day we shall find universities conferring degrees 'while you wait,' as it were. A man, for instance, visiting Boston for a week will some day be able to run out to Harvard, pay a small fee, pass an examination, and get a bachelor's degree, as a sort of souvenir of his visit; another chap, coming to New York for a brief holiday, instead of stealing a spoon from the Waldorf for his collection of souvenirs, can ring up Columbia College, tell 'em all he knows over the wire, and get a sheepskin by return mail; while at New Haven you'll be able to stop off at the railway station and buy your B.

A. at the lunch-counter—they may even go so far as to let the newsboys on the train confer them without making the applicant get off at all. Then the golden age of education will begin. There'll be more college graduates to the square inch than you can now find in any ten square miles in Massachusetts, and our professional men, instead of beginning the long wait at thirty, will be in full practice at twenty-one."

"That is the limit!" ejaculated Mr. Brief.

"Oh, no indeed," said the Idiot. "There's another step. That's the gramophone course, in which a man won't have to leave home at all to secure a degree from any college he chooses. By tabulating his knowledge and dictating it into a gramophone he can send the cylinder to the university authorities, have it carefully examined, and receive his degree on a postal-card within forty-eight hours. That strikes me as being the limit, unless some of the ten-cent magazines offer an LL. D. degree with a set of Kipling and a punching-bag as a premium for a one year's subscription."

"And you think that will be a good thing?" demanded the Bibliomaniac.

"No, I didn't say so," said the Idiot. "In one respect I think it would be a very bad thing. Such a method would involve the utter destruction of the football and rowing seasons, unless the universities took some decided measures looking toward the preservation of these branches of undergraduate endeavor. It is coming to be recognized as a fact that a man can be branded with the mark of intellectual distinction in absentia, as the Aryan tribes used to put it, but a man can't win athletic prowess without giving the matter attention in propria persona, to adopt the phraseology of the days of Uncle Remus. You can't stroke a crew by mail any more than you can stroke a cat by freight, and it doesn't make any difference how wonderful he may be physically, a Yale man selling dry-goods out in Nebraska can't play football with a Harvard student employed in a grocery store at New Orleans by telephone. You can do it with chess, but not with basket ball. There are some things in university life that require the individual attention of the student. Unless something is done by our colleges, then, to care for this very important branch of their service to growing youth, the new scheme will meet with much opposition from the public."

"What would you, in your infinite wisdom, suggest?" asked the Doctor. "The wise man, when he points out an objection to another's plans, suggests a remedy."

"That's easy," said the Idiot. "I should have what I should call residential terms for those who wished to avail themselves of athletic training under academic auspices. The leading colleges could announce that they were open for business from October 1st to December 1st for the study of the Theory and Practice of Gridirony—"

"Excuse me," said Mr. Pedagog. "But what was that word?"

"Gridirony," observed the Idiot. "That would be my idea of the proper academic designation of a course in football, a game which is played on the gridiron. It is more euphonious than goalology or leather spheroids, which have suggested themselves to me."

"Go on!" sighed the Doctor. "As a word-mint you are unrivalled."

"There could be a term in baseballistics; another in lacrossetics; a fourth in aquatics, and so on all through the list of intercollegiate sports, each in the season best suited to its completest development."

"It's not a bad idea, that," said Mr. Pedagog. "A parent sending his boy to college under such conditions would have a fairly good idea of what the lad was doing. As matters are now, it's a question whether the undergraduate acquires as much of Euripides as he does of Travis, and as far as I can find out there are more Yale men around who know all about Bob Cook and Hinkey than there are who are versed in Chaucer, Milton, and Shakespeare."

"But what have these things to do with the arts?" asked Mr. White-choker. "A man may know all about golf, base and foot ball and rowing, and yet be far removed from the true ideals of culture. You couldn't give a man a B. A. degree because he was a perfect quarter rush, or whatever else it is they call him."

"That's a good criticism," observed the Idiot, "and there isn't a doubt in my mind that the various faculties of our various colleges will meet it by the establishment of a new degree which shall cover the case."

"Again I would suggest that it is up to you to cover that point," said Mr. Brief. "You have outlined a pretty specific scheme. The notion that you haven't brains enough to invent a particular degree is to my mind preposterous."

"Right," said the Idiot. "And I think I have it. When I was in college they used to confer a degree upon chaps who didn't quite succeed in passing their finals which was known as A. B. Sp. Gr.—they were mostly fellows who had played more football than Herodotus who got them. The Sp. Gr. meant 'by special favor of the Faculty.' I think I should advocate that, only changing its meaning to 'Great Sport.'"

Mr. Pedagog laughed heartily. "You are a great Idiot," he said. "I wonder they don't call you to a full professorship of idiocy somewhere."

"I guess it's because they know I wouldn't go," said the Idiot.

"Did you say you were in college ever?" sneered the Bibliomaniac, rising from the table.

"Yes," said the Idiot. "I went to Columbia for two weeks in the early nineties. I got a special A. B. at the beginning of the third week for my proficiency in sciolism and horseplay. I used a pony in an examination and stuck too closely to the text."

"You talk like it," snapped the Bibliomaniac.

"Thank you," returned the Idiot, suavely. "I ought to. I was one of the few men in my class who really earned his degree by persistent effort."

CHAPTER XVI

THE HORSE SHOW

"I SUPPOSE, Mr. Idiot," observed Mr. Brief, as the Idiot took his accustomed place at the breakfast-table, "that you have been putting in a good deal of your time this week at the Horse Show?"

"Yes," said the Idiot, "I was there every night it was open. I go to all the shows—Horse, Dog, Baby, Flower, Electrical—it doesn't matter what. It's first-rate fun."

"Pretty fine lot of horses, this year?" asked the Doctor.

"Don't know," said the Idiot. "I heard there were some there, but I didn't see 'em."

"What?" cried the Doctor. "Went to the Horse Show and didn't see the horses?"

"No," said the Idiot. "Why should I? I don't know a cob from a lazy back. Of course I know that the four-legged beast that goes when you say get ap is a horse, but beyond that my equine education has been neglected. I can see all the horses I want to look at on the street, anyhow."

"Then what in thunder do you go to the Horse Show for?" demanded the Bibliomaniac. "To sleep?"

"No," rejoined the Idiot. "It's too noisy for that. I go to see the people. People are far more interesting to me than horses, and I get more solid fun out of seeing the nabobs go through their paces than could be got out of a million nags of high degree kicking up their heels in the ring. If they'd make the horses do all sorts of stunts, it might be different, but they don't. They show you the same old stuff year in and year out, and things that you can see almost any fine day in the Park during the season. You and I know that a four-horse team can pull a tally-ho coach around without breaking its collective neck. We know that two horses harnessed together fore and aft instead of abreast are called a tandem, and can drag a cart on two wheels and about a mile high a reasonable distance without falling dead. There isn't anything new or startling in their performance, and why anybody should pay to see them doing the commonplace, every-day act I don't know. It isn't as if they had a lot of thoroughbreds on exhibition who could sit down at a table and play a round of bridge whist or poker. That would be worth seeing. So would a horse that could play 'Cavalleria Rusticana' on the piano, but when it comes to dragging a hansom-cab or a grocery-wagon around the tanbark, why, it seems to me to lack novelty."

"The idea of a horse playing bridge whist!" jeered the Bibliomaniac. "What a preposterous proposition!"

"Well, I've seen fellows with less sense than the average horse make a pretty good stab at it at the club," said the Idiot. "Perhaps my suggestion is extreme, but I put it that way merely to emphasize my point. I've seen an educated pig play cards, though, and I don't see why they can't put the horse through very much the same course of treatment and teach him to do something that would make him more of an object of interest when he has his week of glory. I don't care what it is as long as it is out of the ordinary."

"There is nothing in the world that is more impressive than a fine horse in action," said the Doctor. "What you suggest would take away from his dignity and make him a freak."

"I didn't say it wouldn't," rejoined the Idiot. "In fact, my remarks implied that it would. You don't quite understand my meaning. If I owned a stable I'd much rather my horses didn't play bridge whist, because, in all probability, they'd be sending into the house at all hours of the night asking me to come over to the barn and make a fourth hand. It's bad enough having your neighbors doing that sort of thing without encouraging your horse to go into the business. Nor would it please me as a lover of horseback-riding to have a mount that could play grand opera on the piano. The chances are it would spoil three good things—the horse, the piano, and the opera—but if I were getting up a show and asking people from all over the country to pay good money to get into it, then I should want just such things. In the ordinary daily pursuits of equine life the horse suits me just as he is, but for the extraordinary requirements of an exhibition he lacks diverting qualities. He's more solemn than a play by Sudermann or Blanketty Bjornsen; he is as lacking in originality as a comic-opera score by Sir Reginald de Bergerac, and his drawing powers, outside of cab-work, as far as I am concerned, are absolutely nil. A horse that can draw a picture I'd travel miles to see. A horse that can't draw anything but a T-cart or an ice-wagon hasn't two cents' worth of interest in my eyes."

"But can't you see the beauty in the action of a horse?" demanded the Doctor.

"It all depends on his actions," said the Idiot. "I've seen horses whose actions were highly uncivilized."

"I mean his form—not his behavior," said the Doctor.

"Well, I've never understood enough about horses to speak intelligently on that point," observed the Idiot. "It's incomprehensible to me how your so-called judges reason. If a horse trots along hiking his forelegs 'way up in the air as if he were grinding an invisible hand-organ with both feet, people rave over his high-stepping and call him all sorts of fine names. But if he does the same thing with his hind-legs they call it springhalt or stringhalt, or something of that kind, and set him down as a beastly old plug. The scheme seems to me to be inconsistent, and if I were a horse I'm blessed if I think I'd know what to do. How a thing can be an accomplishment in front and a blemish behind is beyond me, but there is the fact. They give a blue ribbon to the front-hiker and kick the hind-hiker out of the show altogether—they wouldn't even pin a Bryan button on his breast."

"I fancy a baby show is about your size," said the Doctor.

"Well—yes," said the Idiot, "I guess perhaps you are right, as far as the exhibit is concerned. There's something almost human about a baby, and it's the human element always that takes hold of me. It's the human element in the Horse Show that takes me and most other people as well. Fact is, so many go to see the people and so few to see the horses that I have an idea that some day they'll have it with only one horse—just enough of a nag to enable them to call it a Horse Show—and pay proper attention to the real things that make it a success even now."

The Doctor sniffed contemptuously. "What factors in your judgment contribute most to the success of the Horse Show?" he asked.

"Duds chiefly," said the Idiot, "and the people who are inside of them. If there were a law passed requiring every woman who goes to the Horse Show to wear a simple gown in order not to scare the horses, ninety per cent. of 'em would stay at home, and all the blue-ribbon steeds in creation couldn't drag them to the Garden—and nobody'd blame them for it, either. Similarly with the men. You don't suppose for an instant, do you, that young Hawkins Van Bluevane would give seven cents for the Horse Show if it didn't give him a chance to appear every afternoon in his Carnegie plaid waistcoat?"

"That's a new one on me," said Mr. Brief. "Is there such a thing as a Carnegie plaid?"

"It's the most popular that ever came out of Scotland," said the Idiot. "It's called the Carnegie because of the size of the checks. Then there's poor old Jimmie Varickstreet—the last remnant of a first family—hasn't enough money to keep a goat-wagon, and couldn't tell you the difference between a saw-horse and a crupper. He gives up his hall bedroom Horse-Show week and lives in the place day and night, covering up the delinquencies of his afternoon and evening clothes with a long yellow ulster with buttons like butter-saucers distributed all over his person—"

"Where did he get it, if he's so beastly poor?" demanded the Lawyer.

"He's gone without food and drink and clothes that don't show. He has scrimped and saved, and denied himself for a year to get up a gaudy shell in which for six glorious days to shine resplendent," said the Idiot. "Jimmie lives for those six days, and as you see him flitting from box to box and realize that he is an opulent swell for six days of every year, and a poor, down-trodden exile for the rest of the time, you don't grudge him his little diversion and almost wish you had sufficient will power to deny yourself the luxuries and some of the necessities of life as well to get a coat like that. If I had my way they'd award Jimmie Varickstreet at least an honorable mention as one of the most interesting exhibits in the whole show.

"And there are plenty of others. There's raw material enough in that Horse Show to make it a permanent exhibition if the managers would only get together and lick it into shape. As a sort of social zoo it is unsurpassed, and why they don't classify the various sections of it I can't see. In the first place, imagine a dozen boxes filled with members of the Four Hundred, men and women whose names have become household words, and wearing on their backs garments made by the deft fingers of the greatest sartorial artists of the ages. You and I walk in and are permitted to gaze upon this glorious assemblage—the American nobility—in its gayest environment. Wouldn't it interest you to know that that very beautiful woman in the lavender creation, wrapped up in a billion-dollar pearl necklace, is the famous Mrs. Bollington-Jones, who holds the divorce championship of South Dakota, and that those two chaps who are talking to her so vivaciously are two of her ex-husbands, Van Bibber Beaconhill and 'Tommy' Fitz Greenwich? Wouldn't it interest you more than any horse in the ring to know that her gown was turned out at Mrs. Robert Bluefern's Dud Studio at a cost of nine thousand seven hundred and fifty dollars, hat included? Yet the programme says never a word about these people. Every horse that trots in has a number so that you can tell who and what and why he is, but there are no placards on Mrs. Bollington-Jones by which she may be identified.

"Then on the promenade, there is Hooker Van Winkle. He's out on bail for killing a farmer with his automobile up in Connecticut somewhere. There is young Walston Addlepate, whose father pays him a salary of twenty-five thousand dollars a year for keeping out of business. There's Jimson Gooseberry, the cotillon leader, whose name is on every lip during the season. Approaching you, dressed in gorgeous furs, is Mrs. Dinningforth Winter, who declined to meet Prince Henry when he was here, because of a previous engagement to dine with Tolby Robinson's pet monkey just in from a cruise in the Indies. And so it goes. The place fairly shrieks with celebrities whose names appear in the *Social Register*, and whose photographs in pink and green are the stock in trade of the Sunday newspapers of saffron tendencies everywhere—but what is done about it? Nothing at all. They come and go, conspicuous but unidentified, and wasting their notoriety on the desert air. It is a magnificent opportunity wasted, and, unless you happen to know these people by sight, you miss a thousand and one little points which are the sine qua non of the show."

"I wonder you don't write another Baedeker," said the Bibliomaniac—"*The Idiot's Hand-book to the Horse Show, or Who's Who at the Garden.*"

"It would be a good idea," said the Idiot. "But the show people must take the initiative. The whole thing needs a live manager."

"A sort of Ward MacAllister again?" asked Mr. Brief.

"No, not exactly," said the Idiot. "Society has plenty of successors to Ward MacAllister. What they seem to me to need most is a P. T. Barnum. A man like that could make society a veritable Klondike, and with the Horse Show as a nucleus he wouldn't have much trouble getting the thing started along."

CHAPTER XVII

SUGGESTION TO CHRISTMAS SHOPPERS

"BY Jingo!" said the Idiot, as he wearily took his place at the breakfast-table the other morning, "but I'm just regularly tuckered out."

"Late hours again?" asked the Lawyer.

"Not a late hour," returned the Idiot. "Matter of fact, I went to bed last night at half-after seven and never waked until nine this morning. In spite of all that sleep and rest I feel now as if I'd been put through a threshing-machine. Every bone in my body from the funny to the medulla aches like all possessed, and my joints creak like a new pair of shoes on a school-boy in church, they are so stiff."

"Oh well," said the Doctor, "what of it? The pace that kills is bound to have some symptoms preliminary to dissolution. If you, like other young men of the age, burn the candle at both ends and in the middle, what can you expect? You push nature into a corner and then growl like all possessed because she rebels."

"Not I," retorted the Idiot. "Mr. Pedagog and the Poet and Mr. Bib may lead the strenuous life, but as for mine the simple life is the thing. I'm not striving after the unattainable. I'm not wasting my physical substance in riotous living. The cold and clammy touch of dissipation is not writing letters of burning condemnation proceedings on my brow. Excesses in any form are utterly unknown to me, and from one end of the Subway to the other you won't find another man of my age who in general takes better care of himself. I am as watchful of my own needs as though I were a baby and my own nurse at one and the same time. No mother could watch over her offspring more tenderly than I watch over me, and—"

"Well, then, what in thunder is the matter with you?" cried the Lawyer, irritated. "If this is all true, why on earth are you proclaiming yourself as a physical wreck? There must be some cause for your condition."

"There is," said the Idiot, meekly. "I went Christmas shopping yesterday without having previously trained for it, and this is the result. I sometimes wonder, Doctor, that you gentlemen, who have the public health more or less in your hands, don't take the initiative and stave off nervous prostration and other ills attendant upon a run-down physical condition instead of waiting for a fully developed case and trying to cure it after the fact. The ounce-of-prevention idea ought to be incorporated, it seems to me, into the materia medica."

"What would you have us do, move mountains?" demanded the Doctor. "I'm not afraid to tackle almost any kind of fever known to medical science, but the shopping-fever—well, it is incurable. Once it gets hold of a man or a woman, and more especially a woman, there isn't anything that I know of can get it out of the system. I grant you that it is as much of a disease as scarlet, typhoid, or any other, but the mind has not yet been discovered that can find a remedy for it short of abject poverty, and even that has been known to fail."

"That's true enough," said the Idiot, "but what you can do is to make it harmless. There are lots of diseases that our forefathers used to regard as necessarily fatal that nowadays we look upon as mere trifles, because people can be put physically into such a condition that they are practically immune to their ravages."

"Maybe so—but if people will shop they are going to be knocked out by it. I don't see that we doctors can do anything to mitigate the evil effects of the consequences ab initio. After the event we can pump you full of quinine and cod-liver oil and build you up again, but the ounce of prevention for shopping troubles is as easily attainable as a ton of radium to a man with eight cents and a cancelled postage-stamp in his pocket," said the Doctor.

"Nonsense, Doctor. You're only fooling," said the Idiot. "A college president might as well say that boys will play football, and that there's nothing they can do to stave off the inevitable consequences of playing the game to one who isn't prepared for it. You know as well as anybody else that from November 15th to December 24th every year an epidemic of shopping is going to break out in our midst. You know that it will rage violently in the last stage beginning December 15th, thanks to our habit of leaving everything to the last minute. You know that the men and women in your care, unless they have properly trained for the exigencies of the epidemic period, will be prostrated physically and nervously, racked in bone and body, aching from tip to toe, their energy exhausted and their spines as limp as a rag, and yet you claim you can do nothing. What would we think of a football trainer who would try thus to account for the condition of his eleven at the end of a season? We'd bounce him, that's what."

"Perhaps that gigantic intellect of yours has something to suggest," sneered the Doctor.

"Certainly," quoth the Idiot. "I dreamed it all out in my sleep last night. I dreamed that you and I together had started a series of establishments all over the country—"

"To eradicate the shopping evil?" laughed the Doctor. "A sort of Keeley Cure for shopping inebriates?"

"Nay, nay," retorted the Idiot. "The shopping inebriate is too much of a factor in our commercial prosperity to make such a thing as that popular. My scheme was a sort of shopnasium."

"A what?" roared the Doctor.

"A shopnasium," explained the Idiot. "We have gymnasiums in which we teach gymnastics. Why not have a shopnasium in which to teach what we might call shopnastics? Just think of what a boon it would be for a lot of delicate women, for instance, who know that along about Christmas-time they must hie them forth to the department stores, there to be crushed and mauled and pulled and hauled until there is scarcely anything left to them, to feel that they could come to our shopnasium and there be trained for the ordeal which they cannot escape."

"Very nice," said the Doctor. "But how on earth can you train them? That's what I'd like to know."

"How? Why, how on earth do you train a football team except by practice?" demanded the Idiot. "It wouldn't take a very ingenious mind to figure out a game called shopping that would be governed by rules similar to those of football. Take a couple of bargain-counters for the goals. Place one at one end of the shopnasium and one at the other. Then let sixty women start from number one and try to get to number two across the field through another body of sixty women bent on getting to the other one, and vice versa. You could teach 'em all the arts of the rush-line, defence, running around the ends, breaking through the middle, and all that. At first the scrimmage would be pretty hard on the beginners, but with a month's practice they'd get hardened to it, and by Christmas-time there isn't a bargain-counter in the country they couldn't reach without more than ordinary fatigue. An interesting feature of the game would be to have automatic cars and automobiles and cabs running to and fro across the field all the time so that they would become absolute masters of the art of dodging similar vehicles when they encounter them in real life, as they surely must when the holiday season is in full blast and they are compelled by the demands of the hour to go out into the world."

"The women couldn't stand it," said the Doctor. "They might as well be knocked out at the real thing as in the imitation."

"Not at all," said the Idiot. "They wouldn't be knocked out if you gave them preliminary individual exercise with punching-bags, dummies for tackle practice, and other things the football player uses to make himself tough and irresistible."

"But you can't reason with shopping as you do with football," suggested the Lawyer. "Think of the glory of winning a goal which sustains the football player through the toughest of fights. The knowledge that the nation will ring with its plaudits of his gallant achievement is half the backing of your quarter-back."

"That's all right," said the Idiot, "but the make-up of the average woman is such that what pursuit of fame does for the gladiator, the chase after a bargain does for a woman. I have known women so worn and weary that they couldn't get up for breakfast who had a lion's strength an hour later at a Monday marked-down sale of laundry soap and Yeats's poems. What the goal is to the man the bargain is to the woman, so on the question of incentive to action, Mr. Brief, the sexes are about even. I really think, Doctor, there's a chance here for you and me to make a fortune. Dr. Capsule's Shopnasium, opened every September for the training and development of expert shoppers in all branches of shopnastics, under the medical direction of yourself and my business management would be a winner. Moreover, it would furnish a business opening for all those football players our colleges are turning out, for, as our institution grew and we established branches of it all over the country, we should, of course, have to have managers in every city, and who better to teach all these things than the expert footballist of the hour?"

"Oh, well," said the Doctor, "perhaps it isn't such a bad thing, after all; but I don't think I care to go into it. I don't want to be rich."

"Very well," said the Idiot. "That being the case, I will modify my suggestion somewhat and send the idea to President Taylor of Vassar and other heads of women's colleges. As things are now they all ought to have a course of shopping for the benefit of the young women who will soon graduate into the larger institution of matrimony. That is the only way I can see for us to build up a woman of the future who will be able to cope with the strenuous life that is involved to-day in the purchase of a cake of soap to send to one's grandmother at Christmas. I know, for I have been through it; and rather than do it again I would let the All-American eleven for 1908 land on me after a running broad jump of sixteen feet in length and four in the air."

CHAPTER XVIII

FOR A HAPPY CHRISTMAS

"I HAVE a request to make of you gentlemen," observed the Idiot, as the last buckwheat-cake of his daily allotment disappeared within. "And I sincerely hope you will all grant it. It won't cost you anything, and will save you a lot of trouble."

"I promise beforehand under such conditions," said the Doctor. "The promise that doesn't cost anything and saves a lot of trouble is the kind I like to make."

"Same here," said Mr. Brief.

"None for me," said the Bibliomaniac. "My confidence in the Idiot's prophecies is about as great as a defeated statesman's popular plurality. My experience with him teaches me that when he signals no trouble ahead then is the time to look out for squalls. Therefore, you can count me out on this promise he wants us to make."

"All right," said the Idiot. "To tell the truth, I didn't think you'd come in because I didn't believe you could qualify. You see, the promise I was going to ask you to make presupposes a certain condition which you don't fulfil. I was going to ask you, gentlemen, when Christmas comes to give me not the rich and beautiful gifts you contemplate putting into my stocking, but their equivalent in cash. Now you, Mr. Bib, never gave me anything at Christmas but advice, and your advice has no cash equivalent that I could ever find out, and even if it had I'm long on it now. That piece of advice you gave me last March about getting my head shaved so as to give my brain a little air I've never been able to use, and your kind suggestion of last August, that I ought to have my head cut off as a sure cure of chronic appendicitis, which you were certain I had, doctors tell me would be conducive to heart failure, which is far more fatal than the original disease. The only use to which I can put it, on my word of honor, is to give it back to you this Christmas with my best wishes."

"Bosh!" sneered the Bibliomaniac.

"It was, indeed," said the Idiot. "And there isn't any market for it. But the rest of you gentlemen will really delight my soul if you will do as I ask. You, Mr. Brief—what is the use of your paying out large sums of money, devoting hour after hour of your time, and practically risking your neck in choosing it, for a motor-car for me, when, as a matter of fact, I'd rather have the money? What's the use of giving thirty-six hundred dollars for an automobile to put in my stocking when I'd be happier if you'd give me a certified check for twenty-five hundred dollars? You couldn't get any such discount from the manufacturers, and I'd be more greatly pleased into the bargain. And you, Doctor—generous heart, that you are—why in thunder should you wear yourself out between now and Christmas-day looking for an eighteen-hundred-dollar fur-lined overcoat for me, when, as a matter of actual truth, I'd prefer a twenty-two-dollar ulster with ten crisp one-hundred-dollar bills in the change-pocket?"

"I'm sure I don't see why I should," said the Doctor. "And I promise you I won't. What's more, I'll give you the ulster and the ten crisp one hundred dollars without fail if you'll cash my check for eighteen hundred dollars and give me the change."

"Certainly," said the Idiot. "How will you have it, in dimes or nickels?"

"Any way you please," said the Doctor, with a wink at Mr. Brief.

"All right," returned the Idiot. "Send up the ulster and the ten crisps and I'll give you my check for the balance. Then I'll do the same by you, Mr. Poet. My policy involves a square deal for everybody whatever his previous condition of servitude. Last year, you may remember, you sent me a cigar and a lovely little poem of your own composition:

> *"When I am blue as indigo, you wrote,*
> *And cold as is the Arctic snow,*
> > *Give me no megrims rotting.*
> *I choose the friend*
> *The Heavens send*
> > *Who takes me Idiyachting.*

Remember that? Well, it was a mighty nice present, and I wouldn't sell it for a million abandoned farms up in New Hampshire, but this year I'd rather have the money—say one thousand dollars and five cents—a thousand dollars instead of the poem and five cents in place of the cigar."

"I am afraid you value my verse too high," smiled the Poet.

"Not that one," said the Idiot. "The mere words don't amount to much. I could probably buy twice as many just as good for four dollars, but the way in which you arranged them, and the sentiment they conveyed, made them practically priceless to me. I set their value at a thousand dollars because that is the minimum sum at which I can be tempted to part with things that on principle I should always like to keep—like my word of honor, my conscience, my political views, and other things a fellow shouldn't let go of for minor considerations. The value of the cigar I may have placed too high, but the poem—never."

"And yet you don't want another?" asked the Poet, reproachfully.

"Indeed I do," returned the Idiot, "but I can't afford to own so much literary property any more than I can afford to possess Mr. Brief's automobile—and this is precisely what I am driving at. So many people nowadays present us at Christmas with objects we can't afford to own, that we cannot possibly repay, and overwhelm us with luxuries when we are starving for our necessities, so that Christmas, instead of bringing happiness with it, brings trial and tribulation. I know of a case last year where a very generous-hearted individual sent a set of Ruskin, superbly bound in full calf that would have set the Bibliomaniac here crazy with joy, to a widow who had just pawned her wedding-ring to buy a Christmas turkey for her children. A bundle of kindling-wood would have been far more welcome than a Carnegie library at that moment, and yet here was a generous soul who was ready to spend a good hundred dollars to make the recipient happy. Do you suppose the lady looked upon that sumptuous Ruskin with anything but misery in her heart?"

"Oh, well, she could have pawned that instead of her wedding-ring," sniffed the Bibliomaniac.

"She couldn't for two reasons," said the Idiot. "In the first place, her sensibilities were such that she could not have pawned a present just received, and, in the second place, she lived in the town of Hohokus on the Nepperhan, and there isn't a pawnshop within a radius of fifty miles of her home. Besides, it's easier to sneak into a pawnshop with a wedding-ring for your collateral than to drive up with a van big enough to hold a complete set of Ruskin bound in full calf. It takes nerve and experience to do that with a cool and careless mien, and, whatever you may have in that respect, Mr. Bib, there are few refined widows in reduced circumstances who are similarly gifted. Then take the case of my friend Billups—some sharp of a tailor got out a judgment against Billups for ninety-eight dollars for a bill he couldn't pay on the fifteenth of December. Billups got his name in the papers, and received enough notoriety to fill him with ambition to go on the stage, and it nearly killed him, and what do you suppose his friends did when Christmas came around? Did they pay off that judgment and relieve him of the odium of having his name chalked up on the public slate? Not they. They sent him forty dollars' worth of golf-clubs, sixteen dollars' worth of cuff-buttons, eight ten-dollar umbrellas, a half-dozen silver match-boxes, a cigar-cutter, and about two hundred dollars' worth of other trash that he's got to pay storage-room for. And on top of that, in order to keep up his end, Billups has had to hang up a lot of tradesmen for the match-cases and cigar-cutters and umbrellas and trash he's sent to his generous friends in return for their generosity."

"Oh, rot," interrupted the Bibliomaniac. "What an idiot your friend Billups must be. Why didn't he send the presents he received to others, and so saved his money to pay his debts with?"

"Well, I guess he didn't think of that," said the Idiot. "We haven't all got the science of Christmas-giving down as fine as you have, Mr. Bib. But that is a valuable suggestion of yours and I'll put it down among the things that can be done in the plan I am formulating for the painless Christmas."

"We can't relieve one another's necessities unless we know what they are, can we?" asked Mr. Whitechoker.

"We can if we adopt my cash system," said the Idiot. "For instance, I know that I need a dozen pairs of new socks. Modesty would prevent my announcing this fact to the world, and as long as I wear shoes you'd never find it out, but if, when Christmas came, you gave me twenty-five dollars instead of Foxe's *Book of Martyrs* in words of one syllable, you would relieve my necessities and so earn my everlasting gratitude. Dr. Capsule here wouldn't acknowledge to you or to me that his suspenders are held together in three places with safety-pins, and will so continue to be until these prosperous times moderate; but if we were to present him with nine dollars and sixty-eight cents on Christmas morning, we should discern a look of gratitude in his eye on that suspender account that would be missing if we were to hand him out a seven-dollar gold-mounted shaving-mug instead. We should have shown our generous spirit on his behalf, which is all a Christmas present ever does, whether it is a diamond tiara or a chain of sausages, and at the same time have relieved his anxieties about his braces. His gratitude would be double-barrelled, and his happiness a surer shot. Give us the money, say I, and let us relieve our necessities first, and then if there is anything left over we can buy some memorial of the day with the balance."

"Well, I think it's a pretty good plan," said Mrs. Pedagog. "It would save a lot of waste, anyhow. But it isn't possible for all of us to do it, Mr. Idiot. I, for instance, haven't any money to give you."

"You could give me something better," said the Idiot. "I wouldn't accept any money from you for a Christmas present."

"Then what shall it be?" asked the Landlady.

"Well—a receipt in full for my bill to date," said the Idiot.

"Mercy!" cried the Landlady. "I couldn't afford that—"

"Oh, yes you could," said the Idiot. "Because for your Christmas I'd give you a check in full for the amount."

"Oh—I see," smiled the Landlady. "Then what do we get for our Christmas? Strikes me it's about as broad as it is long."

"Precisely," said the Idiot. "We get even—and that's about as conducive to a happy Christmas, to Peace on Earth and Good-will to men, as any condition I know of. If I can get square for Christmas I don't want anything else."